Kathleen

A NOVEL

William F. "Bill" Kelly

WILLIAM F. KELLY

ISBN: 978-1-943258-51-2

Edited by: Amy Ashby

Warren publishing

Published by Warren Publishing, Inc.
Charlotte, NC
www.warrenpublishing.net
Printed in the United States

In memory of my mother and her sister.

CHAPTER ONE

Kathleen Larson, the school crossing guard at Hall Kent School for the past twenty years, didn't like getting dressed up like she was in Alaska. She wore her pacific blue LL Bean storm chaser jacket with the fleece liner, a dark blue wool scarf, a fleece hat and insulated gloves all worn over her thermal underwear and usual woolen slacks and flannel shirt. This was the third time she dressed like this in as many days.

Mother Nature was trying to tell her something. The feeling in the pit of her stomach wouldn't go away. It wasn't illness or the flu. The feeling presented itself every time she considered giving up her job. A counseling professional would tell her she was coming to a crossroads and was conflicted as to which road she should take. Maybe some downtime would reward her with the answers she required.

"Stay warm, Mrs. Larson," said the twentieth mother that day as Kathleen opened a car door to allow two children to leave the warmth of the SUV.

She pulled her scarf up to keep the wind from stinging her face, nose, and ears. It was not just the wind; the temperature was below freezing for the third day in a row. This was unusual for the city of Homewood, a suburb of Birmingham, Alabama. There were winters when the temperature would remain above freezing the entire season. The local TV weather people would often predict a light frost, but frequently it didn't come to pass. It was still November, not even officially winter and the weather was playing tricks. She knew this winter would not be normal; no one could convince her there was no such thing as global climate change. The entire world was complaining about unusual weather patterns: warmer summers, droughts, and colder winters. It was climate change for sure, and she was willing to bet one month's salary this winter would be unusual.

The temperature and wind got her thinking again about whether she should retire. As she directed traffic and assisted children from vehicles from the school's circular driveway, she allowed her mind to wander just a bit.

I've put in twenty years, I've got enough money saved and with my small pension and Social Security, I'll be okay. The house is paid for and I require little to be satisfied. Maybe this cold spell is telling me I should be enjoying life a bit more. First thing I'll do is get a new car —maybe go to Key West or take a cruise out of

Miami. That wouldn't be bad. That might even be fun this time of year, and who knows, I might meet a man. I wouldn't know what to do if I did. I'll bet there are people at the Senior Center who would love to travel with me...maybe even a bunch of people. This weather is making me think. Don't tell me there is no such thing as climate change. I'm living it and...

"Hey, Mrs. Larson. Cold enough for yah?" One of the mothers, walking with two kids in tow, was making a poor attempt at humor.

"I'll trade you jobs for the morning," said Kathleen.

She liked being a crossing guard. Two weeks ago, the school district had honored her in the school cafeteria for twenty years of service, by giving her a nice party and catered dinner attended by the mayor and superintendent, and provided a very nice write-up in the Homewood Star, the local newspaper. It wasn't a surprise party, but she was surprised at how many of her friends and parents of present students showed up. There were those who remembered her directing them across the street when they were students at Hall Kent School.

She had never missed a day of work. Even when she was sick or tired, she brought herself to the school to help children depart from the cars and buses. In the afternoon, she helped them cross the street and directed traffic. Not once in the twenty years she'd served had a child been hurt.

Standing next to the superintendent, she'd listened to words of praise about the faithful job she did, day in and day out.

"We have come here tonight to honor Kathleen Larson." These were words she would long remember and cherish. "Crossing guards work without thanks or recognition for very low pay and in most cases, they don't remain long in that position. Besides the poor pay, the job requires you be at your post every morning before school starts and every afternoon before school lets out. Weather is no excuse for being tardy or missing a day, and Mrs. Larson hasn't missed a day in twenty years."

The words of praise and adulation were something she hadn't expected. Mothers and fathers stayed behind to say thanks, bringing tears to Kathleen's eyes.

"Hi, Mrs. Larson," brought her back from her daydream as she helped a child get out of a car and escorted him to the sidewalk. Safety students usually did that job, but they couldn't always keep up when there were multiple children in one SUV. Now several cars required the services of the safety students and Kathleen took up the slack. She was there to make the process go smoothly and to ensure that drivers followed the procedures. Most did but sometimes newcomers or those in a rush wouldn't drive as far forward as they were instructed and traffic would get backed up. Kathleen was always alert to prevent that from happening.

"Have a good day, Emma," she responded to a fourth grader when the child was safely on the sidewalk. In her twenty years at this spot, she was not able to think of one disagreeable incident. Her smile and love of children seemed to be recognized by everyone, all six hundred plus. It seemed like she knew every child by name. One thing was certain, everyone knew Mrs. Larson.

When the children were all in school and the stragglers accounted for, she peeled back the gloves that covered her watch to check the time. One last check and she started the walk back home. There was an alley approximately ten feet wide that saved her about ten minutes of walking. It took her directly from the school on Hall Avenue to Montgomery Lane, where she lived. On each side of the sidewalk was a four-foot high cyclone fence. This made it safe and easy for children on Raleigh Avenue, Montgomery Lane, and Kent Lane to get to school and to reach home quickly if they were walking. A blinking light alerted drivers that children would be crossing the street at these locations.

Once home, she put on the hot water for a cup of tea and peeled off her layers of clothes. These she hung in the closet as she removed them. As she was returning to the kitchen, outside motion caught her eye. Her daughter-in-law was pulling into the driveway in her new black Mustang. It never ceased to annoy her that Tillie bought a vanity tag for the car that said '**MINE.**' She turned toward the front door and unlocked it.

"Hi, Tillie. Just in time for a cup of tea," she said cheerfully as she opened the door. She didn't feel all that cheerful but Tillie was her daughter-in-law, after all.

"Yeah, thanks. I could use a hot cup of tea," Tillie said as she removed her jacket and hat. She dropped these in a heap on the couch and went into the kitchen ahead of Kathleen. Then she got herself a mug from the cabinet, a spoon from the drawer, and the sugar bowl from the sideboard. She didn't wish to wait for her mother-in-law to take her 'sweet old time' getting all these items. Besides, the kettle was whistling.

When Kathleen's son, George, had died five years earlier from heart complications connected with diabetes, Kathleen was lost. Years before, she had adapted to her husband Joseph's death from a heart attack when he returned from the navy, and now she would have to learn to live alone again. She knew she would miss her son. He would faithfully stop by several times each week and repair any of the minor items that needed attending. Sometimes he'd come by simply to say hello. When he died, Tillie took control of the funeral and all the details, and she told Kathleen what to wear and when she would be picked up for the funeral mass. She set up food, snacks, and drinks for all who attended the service at the cemetery and invited everyone back to Kathleen's house, since it was larger than Tillie's apartment.

The day of the funeral, when everyone was gone, Tillie told Kathleen it was time to let her take over her finances. "You have to give me power of attorney. I'm afraid you're not doing your checkbook like you should. Who knows what else needs doing?"

Kathleen had ignored Tillie's attempts to be in charge of her finances, but that was five years ago. Now it was more difficult to handle taking care of the house, finances, insurance, and the electric, water, and gas bills as well as the phone and cable. George had been a big help with a lot of these small chores, and she believed she might need some assistance, though she didn't want it to come from Tillie. She was good about telling her what she needed to do, but not so helpful when Kathleen asked about a bill or didn't understand something. This was why Kathleen didn't trust her and didn't want her to know all her business.

"How much longer will you be able to take care of the house and balance the checkbook and pay for the neighbor boy to mow the lawn? You can't repair a toilet or paint the trim. Who is going to do that?" Tillie was annoying Kathleen with these questions.

"For as long as I'm able, I'll fix them or I'll pay someone to do it. That's why we have plumbers and repair men. With my Social Security check, I'm able to survive. I want to stay in my own home, surrounded by my own things for as long as I can. Just last year I had painters paint the outside of the house. It looks nice and I got a good price."

What Kathleen never told Tillie was that she had insurance money and she'd taken out a policy on George when he was a child, before he got diabetes. She put all the money in a Vanguard mutual fund account and kept the papers hidden in book five of the World Book Encyclopedias that occupied the wall shelf to the left of the television. The other books were mystery, detective, and romance novels and were Kathleen's constant companions. Tillie would never look inside a book. Kathleen was forced to have her taxes prepared professionally each year since; she didn't want Tillie to know any more than she presently knew about her finances. She also had to hide copies of her tax paperwork so Tillie wouldn't snoop at her interest and dividends. She kept the records in a small safety deposit box at the nearest bank on Lakeshore Parkway.

As Tillie rambled on about her work, Kathleen was thinking about life on the beach or a visit to Ireland. *I wonder what life would be like if I quit my crossing guard job. What would I do all day if I didn't have a job to go to? I like walking to and from the school. Besides, the kids all love me and are so respectful. I would miss their cheerful greetings. Their parents recognize and appreciate me. I'm proud of not missing work in twenty years—that's who I am! Now, I'm almost sixty-eight, and as long as I exercise every day, eat right, and stay away from booze, I can live a long and healthy life. Tillie, be damned. My daughter-in-law is not going to tell me how to live or how to spend my money.*

CHAPTER TWO

Tillie often asked Kathleen for a key to the house but Kathleen would remind her that George had told her to guard her keys and not give them to anyone.

"I'm certain he didn't mean me," Tillie replied.

"You're probably right. But in all the time you were married to George, and especially now that he's no longer with us, you have never needed to get in my house. Isn't that true?"

"Yes, but just because I didn't need to in the past doesn't mean I won't in the future. You're not getting any younger, you know. What if you were to fall and you couldn't get up?"

That expression, 'you're not getting any younger,' made Kathleen bristle and Tillie often quoted the commercial that showed an old lady on the floor saying, 'I've fallen and I can't get up.' Nevertheless, Kathleen responded patiently. "We'll deal with that when it happens. I like knowing that no one can get in the house unless I give them a key or they break down the door."

I'm not going to tell Tillie, thought Kathleen, *but I am considering wearing one of those alerts that will call an emergency vehicle should I fall or need help. They don't cost too much and I wouldn't have to call her. I should really look into that.*

Nor was Kathleen about to tell Tillie that she had a key in the backyard shed and if she had to call fire, police, or anyone else because she couldn't get to the door, she would tell them where to find the key. She was also becoming more uncomfortable with Tillie's questions and her renewed efforts to take control. She decided to change the subject.

"Tillie, three times this week I've worn the coat, gloves, and scarf you gave me for Christmas last year. They really kept me warm. I know they were expensive and just because I thanked you once doesn't mean I can't thank you again. I was thankful all morning helping the kids get to their classrooms. I wish I had that jacket several days in past years."

"I'm glad you liked them," Tillie said with a smile. "I never know what I should buy for you. You're difficult to fit, so I'm glad I got something you could use." Tillie always liked getting in a little snide remark about Kathleen's shape. She never missed an opportunity.

Kathleen *was* hard to fit, but she didn't like Tillie always reminding her of it. She was short and plump and built like all the pictures of Mrs. Claus. She had often been compared to the Pillsbury Doughboy and never objected. She was exactly five feet without her shoes, but happy by nature, seldom found fault with people, and truly liked those with whom she came into contact. Tillie was the exception and the one person who could push her buttons. She often wondered what George had seen in her. Then, she didn't have to live with her so she really didn't give a damn. George hadn't been one to complain and so she felt if he was happy, she should be happy for him. Kathleen never used the expression, but she believed "pushy, insensitive bitch"—an expression Tillie used to describe a co-worker—actually described Tillie perfectly. Nevertheless, she was finding it increasingly more difficult to stand up to Tillie. She attributed her cowardice to Tillie's aggression and her own increasing age.

"How come you're not at work today, Tillie?" she asked as Tillie placed her cup in the sink.

"I just needed a day off," Tillie sighed. "I'm accumulating too many vacation days and I haven't used a sick day in a while. So, I called in sick. They don't give a damn. They won't even miss me. Just as long as I catch an occasional cheater once in a while and keep all the clients we presently have, my boss is happy."

Tillie was a supervisor at a health insurance firm. She looked over claims and tried to find ways to save the company money. She would always find ways to deny a claim if she thought she could get away with it. When she found people on the phone who didn't know what was happening, she could often deny a benefit they should have been given, but were too ignorant to understand. She took pleasure in depriving people and liked to brag to Kathleen about how some people never even read their policies and how easy it was to cheat her clients and make her boss happy. Year after year she was recognized as the agent with the highest percentage of profit from the clients she served...or rather, cheated. In Kathleen's opinion, Tillie was not a nice person. She represented the company's interests and her own, but rarely looked out for her clients.

Just before lunch, Tillie decided to go home. Kathleen had offered to feed her, but she declined, saying she had a can of soup at home that she was going to heat up. Kathleen suggested a variety of canned soups, but her daughter-in-law once again declined, saying she needed to get home and feed the cat. Despite her feigned concern, Kathleen was happy to see Tillie go. Besides, her favorite soap was soon to come on television and she preferred not to miss it.

Kathleen's home on Montgomery Lane was modest but adequate. Since it had been repainted a year ago, it was one of the nicest looking houses on the block. She'd had it painted white with a black trim that made the house stand out as neat and clean. While in recent years she didn't do too much gardening, the front yard held an abundance of azaleas, several crepe myrtle trees, and an attractive maple tree. The maple was especially beautiful in the fall when the leaves turned a brilliant red. The yard was relatively low maintenance and only required mowing and edging. Her lawn service kept the house looking tidy.

Inside, the front door opened into the living room. On cold days like today, the living room could get cool very quickly if visitors dallied in the doorway. Several years ago, she'd added a glass door to help keep in the heat in the winter and let the room cool in the summer. The kitchen was straight back, contained a small table where she took all her meals, and opened to a small deck. Off the kitchen was a utility room for the washer and dryer, and a closet with shelves for canned goods. This room had been a dining area, but Kathleen had it made into a utility room so she wouldn't have to go outside to do the laundry. For a small house, the kitchen was generous. Off the hall to the left of the front door were two bedrooms and a bath. And the small car port allowed her to keep her old Buick looking presentable.

The house wasn't big by any stretch of the imagination, but it was adequate, paid for, and comfortable. She knew a handyman who called her frequently to ask if she needed any help. Recently, she'd had him insulate the attic and around the doors and windows and she could tell that the house was not as drafty.

Kathleen kept her relationship with the handyman a secret from Tillie. She wasn't certain why she did it, but withholding that information gave her a strange kind of pleasure. Josh, the young repair man, was more than happy to stop by when she needed him. He often found other items that needed repair and his prices were more than reasonable. He claimed Kathleen was his only act of charity and hoped she wouldn't take that away from him. She decided to keep her relationship with Josh a secret for as long as she could. In fact, the less she told Tillie, the better she felt about herself.

The silence that followed became uncomfortable for Tillie. She liked being the center of attention and felt ignored when Kathleen retreated into her thoughts. She got up from the couch and announced that she needed to go home and feed the cat.

After Tillie headed home to her soup and her cat, Kathleen thought to herself. *No, I like where I live, I like my home, and I'm happy with my life. I don't want to admit it, but I would be happier if Tillie was not part of my existence. This is my life, my home, and I don't want anything more. I am mistress of my castle.*

CHAPTER THREE

On Wednesdays, Kathleen had a standing date to play bridge at the Senior Center. That was one of the few times during the week when she drove her Buick. She drove to bridge, used it for grocery shopping, going to church, and visits to the library. If someone were to check the mileage carefully, it would probably only amount to twenty or twenty-five miles a week. The car was old, but it had very few miles on it and was in first class condition.

"Hey, Kay. We're all here." Her friend Elsie greeted her when she came into the card room.

"Let's draw for partners," Kathleen said, as she spread a deck of cards in a line on the table.

Holly was already sitting at the table and needed no encouragement to draw. She drew a six of diamonds, Elsie drew a seven of clubs, and Marcie a ten of spades. Kathleen hung her coat over a chair at the next table and drew a king of hearts.

"I hope that will be an indication of the cards I get this week. I'll be your partner, Marcie," she said.

Kathleen sat down opposite Marcie and began dealing the cards that had already been shuffled. The ritual of choosing who would play with whom and which player would deal had been established years ago and didn't change with the weather or a substitute. They let the cards decide.

Kathleen liked this group. They all played at a reasonably high level and seldom made mistakes. Nor were they upset if they or their partner did something dumb. They played hard to win, doubled when they thought the opponent couldn't make the bid, and didn't get terribly upset if they misplayed the hand.

After the first hour, both teams made a rubber and were less than a hundred points apart. They took a break to get coffee or a soft drink provided by the Senior Center. Kathleen drank a 7-UP.

Marcie and Kathleen got no points in the next round while Holly and Elsie bid three-no-trump twice and made both contracts, giving them seven hundred bonus points. The last half hour before lunch turned out to be better for Kathleen and Marcie.

Marcie opened with one heart, telling her partner she had five hearts and at least thirteen points. Kathleen had an opening hand, jumped to three hearts and she and Marcie ended up at a small slam, which they made. When the group added up the scores, that last hand made Marcie and Kathleen winners.

All four ladies ate lunch at the center. Kathleen liked that she didn't have to go home and heat something up. Most of the time the meals were acceptable and there was usually more food than she liked to eat. Some days there was a speaker after lunch or a presentation by a doctor from Brookwood Hospital. She especially appreciated the demonstration on how to use your cell phone. Several days a week there were exercise classes, but Kathleen felt she got enough exercise walking twice a day to and from the school. After she'd had a chance to visit with a few of her friends, she drove the Buick home to get ready for her crossing job.

CHAPTER FOUR

*I*t was Friday afternoon and Kathleen was directing
traffic on Hall Avenue and Cobb Street where the
traffic enters the front entrance to the school. The
weather was a balmy seventy degrees, a treat after the
recent cold spell. Seven stations were set up and drivers
were notified by bull horn as to where their child would
be waiting. Parents would display their number through
the front window for the man directing traffic and he
would assign the driver the next available spot. He
called out the numbers one by one in steady rhythm,
"346-2, 267-3, 539-4...." It was the crossing guard's
responsibility to keep the flow of cars steady and to stop
the flow of cars when walkers needed to cross the street.

For the last twenty years, Kathleen had done her
job without incident. Over the years, there were a
few minor adjustments to make the task safer or
to eliminate bottlenecks, but for the most part, the
procedure was unchanged. She saw the task of safely
crossing the walkers, whether children or parents, as
her top priority.

Kathleen had been on the job for about half an hour and was just starting to cross a child, when a mother in a blue SUV—talking on her cell phone, of course—failed to see her in time. Kathleen motioned for the child to stay on the sidewalk and tried to get out of the way. The driver hit the accelerator instead of the brakes and with a terrible squeal the SUV hit Kathleen and sent her sprawling to the curb. The child wasn't hurt but came running to Kathleen and wrapped her little arms around Kathleen's neck, saying over and over, "Mrs. Larson, are you all right?"

Several parents came to Kathleen's aid and the man with the bullhorn told everyone to step back and not try to move her. He took control and kept her safe. Kathleen lay on the street with her leg at a strange angle, her face clearly expressing the pain she was experiencing. She ran her hand over her eyes and face in an effort to make the pain go away. Blood was oozing from her left elbow and her jacket was ripped. Someone called 911 and, several minutes later, an ambulance arrived on Cobb Street. The child was still crying when the paramedics arrived.

The woman who was responsible for the accident got out of the car when the police arrived and, according to another parent, was still talking on the phone as the police took accounts of what happened.

"The lady in the blue SUV was talking on the phone, even after she got out of the car. She wasn't paying attention," the fourth grader told the police.

When the woman saw Kathleen on the gurney, she became upset and started to cry. She came over to the ambulance as Kathleen was being lifted aboard and told her that she was sorry.

Pain radiated through Kathleen's right leg. "I can stand the pain so long as my leg isn't moved," she told the paramedics and winced as they placed her leg in a temporary splint. The ambulance rushed her to Brookwood Hospital where a doctor determined her leg was broken and had to be set. An hour later, her leg immobilized and in a cast and her arm bandaged, Kathleen was finally able to rest comfortably. It was another hour before she could be released from the hospital.

When George had died, Kathleen was forced to list Tillie as her nearest relative. She had two grandchildren who were married, but they didn't live in town, nor did either pay much attention to their grandmother. One lived in Anniston and the other in Pell City. The hospital called Tillie at work and requested she come and get her mother-in-law at the hospital. Of course, they wouldn't release Kathleen until arrangements for payment were made, so she presented her medical cards shortly after Tillie arrived. Then she was given a walker and was released into Tillie's care. The hospital gave Tillie a list of people who could provide home care if Kathleen needed assistance.

Word spread quickly about the accident where Kathleen lived on Montgomery Lane. Her neighbors were wonderful. People brought food and asked if they could get anything. Kathleen asked her next-door neighbor, Elaine Hunt, to go to Homewood Pharmacy to pick up a pain prescription. When Elaine delivered the medicine, she did the dishes and sat with Kathleen. The medicine made her sleepy and she relaxed for the rest of the afternoon and into the evening in her recliner, drifting in and out of sleep. After the initial pain from the accident, she was not in serious discomfort—she attributed that to the pain medicine. Rose Wagner, two houses down, brought a noodle and tuna casserole for supper and stayed with her while she ate. Later, the television kept her company until she fell asleep. She decided to sleep in the recliner, at least this first night.

Tillie came by on Saturday about mid morning. Kathleen had already made coffee and had eaten a bowl of cereal before she arrived. She was doing well by herself, with the help of her walker.

"Mom, we need to talk." Tillie was going to make this conversation a production. She pulled up a chair and made a big display of sitting down at the kitchen table.

"Go ahead, talk," said Kathleen. "I'm anxious to hear what you have to say."

"I need to take over your finances. You need someone to watch over you for your own sake. I should have power of attorney so that I can act on your behalf if an accident like this were to happen again." Tillie paused but had no intention of letting Kathleen speak. "At the hospital, I was treated like a friend to drive you home. I had no say in what they were going to do."

"You didn't need a say. They took an x-ray and told me my leg was fractured and they were going to set it and put it in a cast. I told them to go ahead. Then they bandaged my arm and told me they would keep me in observation for a while. That's all they did and that's all they needed to do. There was no need to call you except for a ride home. What did you want to do?" Kathleen scratched her thigh above her cast, growing increasingly irritated with Tillie.

"This isn't about yesterday. What if you couldn't talk or you were unconscious or you needed someone to sign for an operation? Someone needs to be able to speak for you and do what you want done. It wasn't serious this time...but it could have been," Tillie said with an air of melodrama.

While Tillie was talking, Kathleen was harboring other thoughts. *First of all, you say it wasn't serious. How would you know? You didn't get hit by a car and have your leg broken. You would be the last person I'd want to make decisions as to what is best for me. I don't believe you would always act in my best interest. I'll make my own decisions, thank you.*

"Tillie, I hear what you're saying and maybe I do need someone to speak for me if I'm injured. I'm just not ready to do that." She paused for a moment. "I'll think about it. I need to think about it."

"What *I* need, Mom, is the power of attorney. That would allow me to do what is best for you. Sooner or later someone is going to have to help you and I'm the nearest relative. The kids are too far away and besides they have their own lives. They're busy. Let me help."

"I told you I would think about it. Now why don't you relax and have some coffee?"

The rest of the morning was pleasant enough, but Kathleen's mind was racing. *Tillie is acting as if she cared,* she thought. *She's the nearest relative? Sure, but only by proximity. My grandchildren, Paul and Patti, are my two nearest blood relatives. I'm not all that certain Tillie would do what is best for me. I don't trust her, and, I'm not sure why, but I hate it when Tillie calls me 'Mom.'*

Kathleen also had one other relative—George's ex-wife, Carol. Carol was a sweetheart and the best thing to ever happen to her son. He just hadn't appreciated what he had and when the kids were almost out of high school, he became involved with Tillie. Carol told him to break it off, and while she believed he tried, Tillie wouldn't let go. He couldn't make a decision and Carol was forced to make it for him. Kathleen felt that living with Tillie drove him to an early grave, but of course she would never voice that idea to Tillie. Maybe she needed to talk with Carol.

While her thoughts were on Carol, the phone rang. It was Carol inquiring about her broken leg.

"Hey, Kay! Thanks for leaving that message. Can I come over and see you this evening?"

"I'd love to have you visit. I'll be here all evening and night...as if I could go anywhere."

"Good, I'll see you after work," said Carol.

Moments later, Tillie got up and announced she needed to get going. "I've got to get to my office. I have a few calls to make. "

Kathleen knew Tillie was declaring her displeasure with Carol coming over. *The last thing Tillie would want is for Carol to have power of attorney. That would really frost her,* Kathleen thought as she suppressed a grin.

"Give it some thought about me having the power of attorney," Tillie said as she walked to the door. "Next time someone may have to make decisions, and you'll want someone who will do what's best for you."

She blew a kiss toward Kathleen and left abruptly. Tillie was as easy to read as a nursery rhyme.

CHAPTER FIVE

Carol arrived shortly after seven in the evening. She brought a ray of sunshine the moment she entered the house. "Kay!" she exclaimed, as she embraced her ex-mother-in-law. "What the hell were you doing? Trying to kick that car?"

"I was just trying to get it to slow down. Did you know that lady was talking on her cell phone? Even when she got out of the car and asked if I was hurt, she was still talking. I heard her say, 'I'll call you back, Jane,'" Kathleen said, rolling her eyes.

"Kay, you need a lawyer. You'll be getting a call from the insurance company. They're going to want you to settle."

"And I want to settle. There's no reason not to settle," Kathleen said assuredly.

"Of course not. But do you know what this is costing you?"

"I know I'll not be able to work for a few weeks, but that's about it."

"Wrong." Carol shook her head. "You may be out of commission for six weeks or more and you have an emergency room bill, ambulance and doctor bills that won't show up possibly for a month or two. Not everything will be covered by Medicare." Carol laid her coat on the empty chair in the living room. "You may need physical therapy and that's not cheap. And you don't know if you'll be able to stand on that leg. Nor do you know if you'll be able to walk like you used to or do all the things you did before the accident. That driver may have, by her carelessness, taken that job away from you and changed your entire life situation." Carol placed a hand on Kathleen's shoulder. "You might even feel pain in that leg every time it rains."

"I hadn't thought of that," Kathleen said, once again scratching at her cast. "The school principal came out while I was waiting for an ambulance and told me she would tell administration I was in the hospital. She got the janitor to finish the day for me."

"You don't know. They might not want you to work because you were hurt and they might consider that age had something to do with it. Also, that crazy woman bears some responsibility for using her cell phone while driving. She could have killed you or one of the children. What if you'd broken your hip or were bed ridden for several months...or more? In the next few months, other problems might present themselves...problems that are masked now by the pain killers. Kathleen, you need a lawyer."

Kathleen nodded. Carol always gave the best advice. "Tillie was here and she didn't say a word about a lawyer. All she wanted was for me to give her power of attorney."

"Don't do it, Kay." Carol always called her mother-in-law by her first name since she first met her son. While they were a generation apart in age, they were sisters in spirit. Kathleen liked being called 'Kay' by her former daughter-in-law. It was like she was talking with her sister. "Once Tillie gets you to sign that paper giving her power of attorney, who knows what she'll do. You'll belong to her. I mean that literally."

Kathleen watched Carol go about making tea in the kitchen. She was a big woman, about five nine and a bit overweight. Her hair was dyed red and she kept it cut short. What one would remember about Carol was that she always had a smile on her face and loved to make jokes and wise cracks. Yet you instinctively knew she would be there if you needed her. Kathleen considered her a real sweetheart and enjoyed her visits.

Tea and supper made and Kathleen's leg comfortably propped, Carol switched channels until they found a football game. Kathleen was looking forward to the game that evening between Alabama and Florida and she knew it was also on her daughter-in-law's agenda. They watched the game with the sound on low as they continued to talk until Kathleen started to yawn. She was getting tired, most likely the result of medication. At halftime, Carol got her coat, kissed Kathleen on the cheek, and said as she was going out the door, "Just don't sign away your life. In fact, don't sign anything. If you need me, call."

CHAPTER SIX

*K*athleen spent the next several days in front of the tube watching and growing weary of soaps, sitcoms, and movies. She was also exhausted with listening to the news. But it was the commercials that annoyed her the most and forced her to turn the sound down or turn off the set. The mute button became her best friend.

She wanted her job back.

The knock on the front door forced her to reach for her walker and look out the window to see who it was. There was a distinguished looking man in a black suit standing on the porch. She opened the wooden door.

"Hello? How may I help you?" she said from behind the locked glass door.

"Mrs. Larson, I'm from the school district. May I speak with you?"

Kathleen decided he looked harmless. He was dressed like a preacher, had grey hair mixed with black, and was pleasant when he spoke. He had a black briefcase in his left hand. She wasn't expecting anyone from the school district, but thought it nice that they'd sent someone to visit her. She opened the glass door and invited him in.

"Again, I'm from the school district and, if I may, I would like to ask you some questions about the accident." He stopped just long enough to take a breath before he continued. "I'm sorry you were hurt. First of all, how are you doing?"

Kathleen thought it was nice of him to ask how she was doing. She told him her leg was healing and she was learning to get around using the walker. She thanked him for his concern, although she wondered just how concerned he really was. He looked around the room and didn't appear too interested in her. He asked how the accident happened and how many accidents she'd had previously.

"I've been working as crossing guard for twenty years and have never had an accident," she said, smiling a bit uneasily. "The woman was on the phone. She wasn't paying attention. How many accidents has she had?"

"I'm sorry, Mrs. Larson. I didn't mean to upset you. I just want to know what happened." Kathleen continued to doubt the sincerity of this man. "May I ask you, are you planning to return to work?"

"When my leg is completely healed, it is my intention to return to the job I've been doing for the past twenty years," she said sternly.

"That's good. I have a paper here I need to ask you to sign. It allows the hospital to release the medical records on your leg. We need to know if they believe you are fit for work."

"If I'm not fit for work, I'll quit!" she snapped. Then, clearing her throat she added, "If I can't stand on my leg, I'll have to retire. As long as I'm fit, I'll go to work." Kathleen was beginning to get annoyed with this jerk. She glanced at the form, read it quickly, and signed it.

"I don't want to take up any more of your time," the man said, without making eye contact. "I'll let myself out so you don't have to get up. I hope you recover quickly." He put the paper in his briefcase and left.

When Kathleen spoke with Carol around five o'clock that evening, she casually mentioned she'd received a visit from the school district. Carol responded in a way Kathleen hadn't expected.

"Look, Kay, I can't leave work now but I'll come over to the house as soon as I get off. I know claims, and I'll bet you this guy is not from the school district." Kathleen nodded silently as she listened to Carol. "He's from the insurance company," Carol continued, "if my instincts are correct. Do you have any food in or should I bring some Chinese?"

"No, please. I have plenty of food. The neighbors have been taking great care of me. You'll have several choices. See you when you get here."

It was five-twenty when Carol arrived. She went to the refrigerator and scouted the possibilities before heating up kirsch and a string bean casserole in the microwave. The two ladies ate off TV trays in the living room while listening to the five-thirty news. Carol drank a Diet Coke and Kathleen an iced tea.

Carol worked at the University of Alabama Hospital as a physical therapist. She was often the person they called upon to straighten out a claim. She had good a reputation with both the insurance company and patients.

When the news was over, Carol turned down the television and asked Kathleen why she signed the paper.

"All they wanted to know was if my leg was healed. Why shouldn't they have that information?" Kathleen asked.

"That's not all they wanted. Did he leave a copy of what you signed with you?" Kathleen shook her head. Carol sighed. "They now can find out everything about you. How many operations you may have had, what kind, when and what the prognosis was for other problems. They might consider you a liability and not rehire you back, not because of your leg but because you have diabetes or a heart problem or high blood pressure or who knows what. You've given them permission to examine not just your leg, but you."

"I didn't know they could do that." Kathleen frowned.

"They can't. Except you gave them permission," Carol said with irritation in her voice. "Do you know who it was who came to the house? Was he from the insurance company?"

"I think he said he was from the school district but I'm not really certain. No, he said he was from the school district. He said it twice...when he first knocked on the door and just before he asked me what happened." Kathleen's memory wasn't as sharp as it was when she was younger.

"Did he leave a card?" Carol asked. She could be almost pushy when she was looking out for Kathleen, but for some reason, Kathleen didn't mind it as much as when Tillie pushed her.

"No. And if he told me his name I wouldn't remember it."

"I'm not certain, but I'll bet you twenty bucks to your one that he was from the insurance company and didn't want you to know. He's going to use that information against you if it goes to court or if it will give him an advantage in negotiating a settlement. Kathleen, I've said it before and I'll say it again: you need an attorney."

"Can you get one for me? I wouldn't know where to begin," Kathleen said, wringing her hands.

"Tomorrow, I'll start checking. I have a few friends who are attorneys. Don't worry, we'll see what we can do to limit the information he gets."

After Carol left, Kathleen slumped in her recliner. *I feel a lot better since my conversation with Carol*, she thought. *Sometimes I'm surprised how ignorant I can be. I was brought up in a gentler time when life wasn't so cut throat. I will have to be more cautious and not trust people so easily. I wonder if maybe Tillie was right. Perhaps I am in need of someone who can help me in situations like this. No, no.* She shook her head. *I'm not going to give Tillie power of attorney.*

CHAPTER SEVEN

Carol arrived at her office promptly at eight, got her coffee, looked at some of the new files that showed up on her desk, and searched her phone list for her lawyer friend. She and Jack had been good friends when they both took a college course at the University.

"Hey, Jack. This is Carol. I need some help."

"Sure. What can I do?"

"My mother-in-law needs a lawyer. She's a crossing guard at a school in Homewood and someone hit her with their car and broke her leg. I believe an insurance agent misrepresented himself and she needs someone to protect her rights." She couldn't believe the words as she spoke them.

"Carol, I can't talk now," Jack Martin said as a conversation in the background grew louder. "But I know of a new lawyer in our firm who would be perfect. I'll have him call. Give me your number."

Carol gave him her work number and hung up. Within five minutes, her phone rang and Jack called back. "His name is Andrew Stephens. He'll call you in a few minutes. He's new, he's smart, and he needs a case. He just passed the bar recently and I believe he will do a good job for you." Jack had a pointed way of speaking that put Carol at ease. She'd played with him on the hospital softball team many years ago and except for the gray hair and extra pounds, he remained the same friendly person.

"I'm going to have to rely on you as I wouldn't know how to evaluate a lawyer. If you say he's good, I'll take your word."

"Maybe you two can meet over lunch," Jack offered. "Those insurance guys like to get a head start and get all the information they need before anyone else. The sooner Andrew gets started on this, the better."

Andrew Stephens called ten minutes later and rather than talk on the phone, suggested they meet at a fast food place just a few blocks from where Carol worked. That pleased Carol since she often ate at Captain D's anyway. This attorney sounded like he was down to earth, even if he was new to the profession.

Andrew was dressed in a black suit with a white shirt and dark red tie. It appeared he was told to dress that way since his haircut suggested he was more inclined toward the outdoor hike and bike lifestyle. His complexion and hands said he'd spent last weekend outdoors and one question from Carol confirmed her suspicion. He was either six feet or an inch shorter and looked like he needed a good meal. Carol was reminded of the pictures she saw of a young Abe Lincoln when he was starting his career in Illinois—tall and gaunt. The big difference was Andrew had no facial hair and was good looking. When he smiled, you wanted to smile with him.

They each ordered the shrimp meal with a Coke. She told Andrew about the accident and the subsequent visit by the lawyer. He listened and took a few notes in a small black notebook.

"Carol, first of all, please call me Drew," he said with a toothy smile. "Then give me a dollar as a retainer. How old is your mother-in-law?"

"Sixty-eight, I believe," said Carol. "I could be off a year."

"And what school did she work at?"

Drew went through these preliminary questions, writing the results in his black book.

"I'll call Mrs. Larson this afternoon and will try to find out who was seeking the information about her medical records," he said after he'd completed his questioning. "Also, I'd like to meet her as soon as possible. How about we meet after you get off work tonight?"

"That would be fine," Carol nodded. She appreciated his no-nonsense attitude. "Here's her address. I'll be there about five-fifteen."

Andrew was parked on the street when Carol arrived and together they approached the house. Carol knocked and Kathleen yelled the door was open. Carol entered, followed by Andrew and they both sat on the couch next to her chair. Carol introduced her mother-in-law to the young attorney.

"Mrs. Larson, I found out a few things this afternoon," he said, shaking her hand.

"Please call me Kathleen or Kay," she smiled. "If you're going to be my attorney, you can't call me Mrs. Larson. Choose Kay or Kathleen."

"Okay, Kathleen it is. I'm Drew. I found out it was the insurance company for the lady who hit you that was seeking your medical information. The hospital gave some information about setting the leg but has not yet received the permission letter you signed. It was probably sent by snail mail. I told them they could not give out any medical information and that I would bring a letter for them stating so in the morning. Please sign here, Kathleen. Carol, please witness the signature." Drew left a duplicate copy of the document with Kathleen as well as his business card.

Once the legal stuff was taken care of, the three talked about the prognosis for recovery and whether Kathleen would be able or would want to return to work. It was also agreed that Drew would receive 30% of any cash settlement. Drew said he would insist that the insurance company be required to pay all medical bills in addition to any cash settlement for as long as necessary.

The three talked for a while more before Drew made a move to leave. "I'll be at the hospital at eight in the morning to give them this letter before your first signature gets there."

"Can I ask you a question before you go?" asked Kathleen.

"Sure. I'll try to help in any way I can. What's on your mind?"

"Do I need someone to have power of attorney?"

"I don't know. Are you having any trouble remembering or are you going to sell your house or car? How old are you?"

"I'm sixty-seven. I'll be sixty-eight in April—another five months."

"Have you enrolled in Medicare?"

"Yes. The city pays a portion of my Medicare. They pay a portion of part C," Kathleen responded with concern.

"Good. I think you're in good shape for now," Drew said with an assuring smile. "That's not an immediate problem. Maybe someone needs to have limited power of attorney, but let's take care of the immediate problem. As I get to know you better, I'll be in a position to make an informed decision. When this problem is resolved, we can discuss that." He handed Kathleen a copy of the forms she signed moments before.

Drew patted her on the shoulder, put the forms in his briefcase, said goodbye to Carol and Kathleen, and left. Both ladies agreed he was a nice young man. Kathleen said she had confidence in him and, while she didn't expect any money from the accident, she would not be adverse to a settlement, just in case she couldn't work or there were complications. After all, she did need a new or at least a *newer* car. Her old Buick was showing signs that it was nearing time for costly repairs.

After Carol left, Kathleen watched a cop show, brushed her teeth, and retired, with the feeling she was in safe hands. It was only nine o'clock and she had a lawyer who could be trusted and would act in her best interests. She picked up Andrew's business card from the end table next to the couch. She was sure he could be trusted and was thankful Carol had shown concern and acted in her best interest.

CHAPTER EIGHT

*D*rew, dressed in a black suit with a crisp, white shirt and blue tie, entered the hospital the following morning. He looked every bit the veteran professional. It was several minutes before eight and he had to wait a short time before they opened the administration office. He spoke with the woman with whom he had spoken the day before; a woman with 'Leticia' on her badge. She looked at the document.

"Did he say he was from the Homewood School District?" Drew asked, referring to the gentlemen who'd asked Kathleen to sign the release papers.

"Yes, he did. I remember it because we never get requests from the school district," replied Leticia. She was about twenty-five, well dressed, stocky with an inviting smile. "Unless that gentleman can show me a document dated after this one, I'll not give him access to any medical records," she added with authority.

"You can tell him about the broken leg, since he knows about that injury already, but Kathleen Larson doesn't want you to release any information about her health," Drew said sternly. "I'm going to leave my card with you. Please call after he visits. Tell me if he identifies himself as an employee with the Homewood School District. That would be fraud, so this is critical. Ask him for his card and identification. The letter he sent via snail mail should arrive today. It should have the insurance company's name on it. If you will make a copy of the letter, I would appreciate knowing who is perpetrating these lies."

Drew's next visit was to the school board. He wished to speak with those in insurance to find out what they were willing to do for their employee, Mrs. Larson. He expected the school board to assure her that she had a job when she was ready and able to return to work.

Drew drove to the Homewood School Board office and made inquiries at the information desk as to where he should go. After several stops along the way, he believed he was where he needed to be.

A sign by the door read 'INSURANCE.' The lady inside waved him in while she finished her phone conversation. She pointed to a seat in front of her desk. She finished her conversation and asked Drew how she could help.

"Kathleen Larson told me someone got her to sign a waiver on her medical information. He indicated that he was from the school board," Drew said.

"Well, that isn't true. We would never request that information. Whoever said he was from the school board was lying," said the heavyset women who could easily pass for fifty. Her name plate read 'Shirley.'

Drew nodded. "Do you think it could be someone from the insurance company?" He sometimes liked to play naïve when he was seeking information. "Would they do something like that?"

"In a heartbeat!" she said emphatically. "That's where you'll find your culprit. It's not our policy to request personal information, and we would consider it unethical to use an accident that wasn't her fault to get medical information we have no right to in the first place. We will send someone to see her and explain what she can expect from us. All her medical bills will be paid and we will deal with our insurance company on those matters. You will represent her interests should the insurance company not wish to give her proper compensation for the pain, suffering, loss of pay, and so forth. I'm glad she has an attorney," said Shirley with sincerity.

"Do you have the police report?" Drew asked.

"Not yet. I believe it will be available tomorrow and it will have the name of the insurance company on it. If you wish, I'll make you a copy," she said as she handed Drew a business card.

"Please. That would be helpful. I'll stop by tomorrow. I do need the name of the insurance company and the name of that agent."

Having made a friend at the Homewood School Administration Office, Drew returned to his office.

CHAPTER NINE

*A*lexander R. King was sitting at his desk, reading a paperback. It was a James Patterson mystery novel, involving the detective Alex Cross. It was an old book he'd just never got around to reading. While he didn't read much, he liked books by James Patterson. He told his secretary to hold all calls. *Nothing important ever comes by way of the phone, anyway,* he thought. *If it's important, it will be in a letter.* He saw the phone light up several times, but shortly thereafter the light on the phone buttons went out. When the lights came on a fourth time, his secretary came over the intercom and told him this woman was not about to give up and it might be wise for him to take the call. Without saying a word, he picked up the phone.

"Dr. Alexander King. How may I help you?" he said, using his most professional voice.

"Dr. King. I'm Tillie Larson from Apex Medical Insurance," Tillie cleared her throat as she continued. "It is my responsibility to check on insurance payments to nursing homes to make sure all claims are legitimate. I have some questions about several of your claims and would like to discuss them with you…personally. When would be a convenient time?"

"What seems to be the problem?" Perspiration collected on Dr. King's brow. "We are very careful about the claims we make."

"I'm sure you are," Tillie said, secretly rolling her eyes. "I believe it would be better if I spoke with you in private. That way we can settle any discrepancies with the least amount of difficulty. Sometimes too many people only confuse the matter and what I have to tell you is better spoken privately. Will three this afternoon be acceptable?" Alexander could now feel the perspiration down his neck.

"Three would be fine," he replied.

He wondered if Tillie knew about his late notifications when a client passed away. Maybe she somehow learned about his lack of proper credentials to run a nursing home. He would just have to wait to find out what prompted this visit.

Tillie used her GPS to find Lakeside Nursing Home. It was located about thirty miles from Birmingham, south of the city in Shelby County. It was a single-story older facility set on a ten-acre piece of property, heavily wooded, and pretty much what people would call "in the country." No lake was visible despite the name 'Lakeside.' A small, wooden sign in need of paint announced that one had arrived at the facility. The sign was visible from the entrance of the macadam driveway and that was the only indication of the home, since the building itself was not visible from the road. A winding road through a heavily wooded pine forest led to a small parking lot, which provided parking for six cars. Tillie could not have found the nursing home without the assistance of her GPS and was grateful she thought to use it.

A sign read 'Deliveries in Rear' and there were no cars in the parking lot, so Tillie drove around back. Behind the nursing home was space for twenty or so cars and a place for trucks to unload. Most likely the parking spaces were reserved for the staff. Tillie turned her Mustang around, returned to the front, and parked. She got out of her car and approached the front door.

Tillie walked slowly toward the huge front door, taking a mental picture of the featureless facility. The door reminded her of the kind seen in horror movies. It was about fifteen feet tall, thick, and fastened with heavy wrought iron hinges. She would not have been surprised if a hunchback greeted her. The sound of the bell seemed to reverberate as if in a huge hall. She waited more than a minute and still no one answered. She was just about to ring again when she heard a key in the lock and the door creaked open. She expected a loud noise, but the lock was surprisingly quiet. A large black woman dressed in a white nurse's uniform opened the door and asked her business.

"I have an appointment with Dr. Alexander King."

"Are you Tillie Larson?" the nurse asked cheerfully.

"Yes."

"I believe he's expecting you."

The nurse led Tillie through the common room where most of the patients were gathered. Tillie didn't have time to look around or to take a tour of the building, but she was able to observe that it was laid out in the shape of an 'H,' with the living quarters located in the four wings. The administration wing was on the opposite side of the front entrance. She noticed that many patients sat at tables, staring straight ahead. There was a stale, musty smell, but the home lacked the expected smell of disinfectant. Several patients walked toward her, arms outstretched, wanting to touch her, give greetings, or tell her their name. Some were in wheelchairs. Most were women, but not all. From what she could determine, all were in various stages of dementia. She was grateful she only had to handle the paperwork for this home and seldom had to visit. This brief encounter was all she wanted to see of Lakeside Nursing Home.

Tillie followed the nurse toward a mirrored wall with a steel door to the right-hand side. It was opened by the use of a keypad. She was ushered into the administration wing and led to the doctor's office, which was halfway down the hall on the right.

Dr. King stood up, thanked the nurse, and indicated a seat for Tillie. He told the nurse to close the door, which she did as she left. "What can I do for you, Mrs.

Larson?" He was not feeling good about this interview and was experiencing a vague feeling of threat.

"You have a nice facility here, Doctor. It is rather isolated, is it not?" Tillie said, avoiding eye contact.

"Yes, I suppose it is. Sadly, with the patients we have, most people would be happy if they didn't have to see their loved ones at all since all are in various stages of mental illness. How may I help you?" Dr. King was attempting to take control of the situation, or at least keep some semblance of authority. Nevertheless, his voice did not emit the necessary confidence.

"I have noticed a slight problem in your bookkeeping." Tillie got right to her reason for the visit. "When a patient dies, it is required that you report the day he or she died. It seems that you are frequently reporting patient deaths the following month, allowing the nursing home to be compensated for an extra month without having to provide services. If twenty patients die in a year's time and you receive their social security payments for an extra month, that's as much as twenty thousand dollars that you're overcompensated. Not knowing the dollar amount of the social security checks forces me to conservatively estimate the compensation at a low figure," Tillie raised her brows as the doctor shifted uncomfortably in his chair.

King started to explain but Tillie put her hand up to indicate he should wait.

"It's better you let me finish." She paused. "I'm the only agent who handles your account. If I sign my name, indicating it's okay to pay, you will be paid. If I wish to stop payment or hold your check for a while to check out a discrepancy, you will not get paid on time. Do you understand, Dr. King?" Tillie loved the power that came with catching customers in a bind.

"Yes, I believe I do," Dr. King said, failing to mask his increasing frustration. "You are attempting to shake me down. You want me to give you a cut."

"No, Doctor, you're wrong. I want to ask a favor of you."

"Oh!" The pause that followed lasted at least ten seconds. "Now that's different," he continued somewhat hesitantly. "What is the nature of that favor?"

"I have a mother-in-law who will need nursing care in the near future. She is of sound mind, age 67, and can dress, shower, and take care of her personal needs."

"Why do you want her to stay here? This center is for Alzheimer's patients and those with severe dementia. All of our patients belong in an institution. Your mother-in-law sounds like she could live in a retirement home or assisted living at most. Wouldn't that suit her better?"

Tillie ignored his question. "Your facility is isolated. Few people visit you, or for that matter, even know where you are located. I want a place that will protect my mother-in-law but not let her have visitors," she said, matter-of-factly. Dr. King frowned as she continued. "I feel as if I have some association with your facility and that you will provide her three meals a day, a place to sleep, and keep her safe. For my part, since she is able to care for herself, dress, eat, and shower, I expect she should pay just half of her social security check. I will send that the first of every month."

Dr. King had found himself in a bind and couldn't say no. "That sounds like a fair arrangement," he said. "Will she cause us any trouble?"

"I don't believe so. She'll not like it here, but if she gets three meals a day, a good night's sleep, and some exercise, I think she'll adjust. My obligation, then, will have been fulfilled," said Tillie. "I'll be able to say that I took good care of her."

"When can we expect this new patient?" said Doctor King, visibly more relaxed.

"The legal arrangements have not yet been made. Once they are, I'll call you. For the time being, limit your overcharging to one month. I can overlook that, but might get in trouble if I overlooked a two-month discrepancy. My supervisor just might catch it if she took her job seriously. Then I would be derelict in my duty and could be subject to scrutiny and we simply can't have that. You understand?" Tillie could feel her pulse quicken and her face flush. She was getting her way.

"I understand. I look forward to your call. Nice doing business with you...ah...Mrs. Larson."

"Call me Tillie." She extended her hand and shook his, abruptly leaving his office.

The nurse who let her in met her as she walked through the common room and let her out. She noticed the patients all walked in slow motion or were sitting at tables doing nothing. Many were talking to themselves. The big, heavy door creaked open and closed with a thud. Behind her, she heard the oversized key turn quietly in the lock.

Tillie sat for a few minutes in her car before turning on the ignition. *I know a lot more about you than you think I do, Doctor,* she thought. She knew, for example, that he'd studied in Grenada, and was not really a doctor. He had worked at several nursing homes and had been investigated for prescribing medications incorrectly—with several cases leading to death. He had even been accused of sedating patients on a continuous basis to keep them placid.

The company that hired King to run Lakeside facility was now being investigated by Tillie's insurance organization, not necessarily to prevent future malpractice, but more so they could tell authorities they were investigating that organization, should they be accused of negligence. If nothing happened that could become embarrassing in the future, all investigations would be dropped—or at least not mentioned.

Tillie chose Lakeside because she figured it would be easy to control King and his staff—after all, he was up to his neck in unethical behavior and would likely be able to do her this one small favor. Plus, the facility was a mere thirty miles away, perfect for keeping an eye on Kathleen—and on King. And should he try to pull anything, she could always blackmail him for playing fast and loose with his patients' death dates.

Overall, Tillie was quite pleased with herself. She was doing her job as a responsible daughter-in-law. *Kathleen will be safe here,* she thought. *Safe from herself and safe from anybody who may try to upset my plans—especially Carol.*

CHAPTER TEN

*D*rew went about his business of seeing to Kathleen's claim against the insurance company. One phone call got him the name of the insurance company from the accident report, Lawrence Insurance, and 'Walter Wilson' as the agent assigned to the case. He spent part of the week talking to witnesses and finding out who 'Jane' was on the other end of the phone when the driver caused the accident.

He also put the insurance company on the defensive about deceiving Kathleen and informed them she was considering filing a lawsuit. They denied ever claiming to be from the school board, but Drew told them he had proof they had lied in the past—and Walter Wilson lied to the administrator at the hospital. Drew threatened to file a separate lawsuit for past discretions, since it was obvious they were not ready to defend themselves. They wanted to get rid of this suit as soon as possible.

When Drew met in person with the insurance representative from Lawrence Insurance, there was a clear display of authority by the representative. He didn't shake Drew's hand, stood up while he showed Drew a seat, and lit up a cigarette without saying a word or asking permission. Drew got up from his chair and headed for the door. "If you're not ready to discuss this case, we'll have to do it the hard way: by litigation."

The manager understood that Drew was serious and he had overplayed his cards, possibly because Drew was so young and he thought he would be intimidated. "I'm sorry for being rude. Please stay."

Drew pointed to the cigarette and requested by sign language that he should put it out. "Your name, sir. With whom am I negotiating?"

"Jack Steele. I'm sorry I didn't introduce myself." Both men sat down at the table.

"Maybe we can agree on a settlement figure to care for Mrs. Lawson should she have difficulties down the road," said Drew.

Jack Steele appeared ready to object, then reluctantly said that would be fine.

Drew mentioned all the items to care for any problems with Kathleen's leg for the next five years, with no objections from Steele. He then suggested that Steele reveal the amount the insurance company was prepared to pay. When Steele suggested fifty thousand, Drew had a difficult time holding back a laugh.

"Mr. Steele, I'm inclined to request maximum compensation given what your client did to alter my client's life, her misuse of her cell phone, the deception by your agent, Walter Wilson, and your failure to bargain in good faith." He paused. "Your company is very fortunate since my client, being the nice hard-working lady she is, has set the price she wants."

"What makes you think I'll accept her offer?" asked Steele.

"Because it's a fair price and you would be stupid to reject it."

"And that figure is?"

"One hundred thousand, plus care and therapy for five years if needed."

"You have a deal and my apology," Steele replied, offering a hand shake.

When all necessary papers were prepared, Drew called Kathleen to request a meeting with her.

"Hi, Kathleen, would you put on some tea?" he asked. "I'd like to visit and I have some news that may interest you. I also have some papers you'll need to sign. Would now be a good time?"

"Now is as good as any," Kathleen responded. "I'm not going anywhere. I'll heat up the water."

While they were drinking tea at the kitchen table, Drew explained some of the terms of the agreement. "You are covered for the next five years should you have any problems with your leg. These include pain, medicine, additional surgery or therapy. You will receive $100,000 in compensation for the broken leg, pain, and potential future problems."

Kathleen's mouth opened. It was all more than she'd expected.

"This is compensation for loss of work, pain and suffering, and possibly loss of livelihood." Drew continued. "You will pay me thirty percent, as agreed upon. If this is acceptable, sign here."

"Drew," Kathleen said, a dazed look on her face.

"Yes, Kathleen?"

"Scoot on over here so I can hug your neck."

Drew smiled and obliged.

"Now you just sit there," Kathleen added. "I have a cheesecake I was saving for a special occasion and I believe I have found the right moment." Using her walker, she went to the freezer. Drew immediately jumped up to help, serving as Kathleen's hands as she told him where she kept the plates and forks. He cut the cake and put a generous portion on each plate before returning to the table.

"People from the school board came last week for a visit," Kathleen said after she'd eaten a hearty bite of cake. "They were nice. They said all my medical bills would be taken care of and if I had any trouble with the insurance company, they would stand by me. They also told me I had as much time as I needed if I wished to return to work."

"How do you feel about returning?"

"I have mixed feelings," Kathleen said, sipping her tea. "I like not having to get dressed so early every morning or having my afternoons interrupted. I now have the money to retire, if I want to. Don't tell my daughter-in-law, not Carol but the evil one, *Tillie,* but I have some insurance money squirreled away that she doesn't know about." Drew's eyes widened as he gestured that his lips were sealed. "With this settlement money, I'll have more than enough to retire. Maybe, while I'm still capable, I could take some trips, do some visiting, and spend some time hanging out with people my age. The Senior Center isn't but a few blocks away."

"That sounds good," said Drew. "I'm glad you've got some compensation money. Enjoy it."

"I'll miss the school children. They have given me so much love and affection." Kathleen started to tear up. "They made me feel useful and valuable to the community. I'm going to miss my job…if I don't return."

Drew smiled and patted her shoulder. "The secret to a happy retirement is to have something to do. If you just sit around all day, you'll soon grow tired of that and have no purpose in life. Start making plans if you want to retire. This is the time to do some traveling if you want to see the world. But it's best to do it with a companion, since it costs twice as much if you travel alone."

The two talked for a while longer, until Drew said he needed to get back to the office. He thanked Kathleen for using him as her attorney and told her to call if he could be of any service. "I'm still your attorney until this is finished to your satisfaction," he added.

Kathleen nodded. "I may call to find out about this power of attorney business. I know the time will come when I'll need someone to watch over my financial and health affairs, but that time doesn't seem to be now. I'll call."

"I'd be glad to arrange it according to your wishes," Drew said. "And I agree with you that Tillie is probably not the person for the job. Consider Carol, though."

"I will," she responded. "I'm glad you agree with me. And by the way, I understand I can have all my bills paid automatically without having to write out a check. Is that correct?" Kathleen liked to feel independent and was thankful for any tips Drew could provide.

"That's right. Do you have automatic deposit for your Social Security check?"

"Yes," Kathleen answered.

"Then we'll set it up so all your bills are paid when they become due and the payment to the credit company will be automatic, as well. That way you won't have to worry about all the different dates when you need to send them off. You'll also save on stamps. We might put an extra thousand or two in your account so we make certain you'll never be overdrawn. How about we set that up after the insurance check clears?"

Kathleen was overwhelmed; Drew had been more helpful than she'd ever imagined. "Sounds great! Thanks, Drew," she said with a big grin. "That will be a big load off my mind. I find it a pain to remember who gets paid on what day. What I usually do is pay all the bills the first week of the month, whether they are due or not. If they're paid automatically, I won't have to worry about all the stamps and checks. The only thing I'll have to do is check each month if my account is going up or down. Tillie will have much less to complain about—and I won't have to see her as often!" She laughed. "See you then." Kathleen kissed her hand and then touched Drew's cheek. He smiled and threw a kiss back as he opened the front door.

CHAPTER ELEVEN

*T*illie parked her car in the public lot across the street and walked to the office building nearby. She wore a modest black dress as if she were a widow coming to take care of unpleasant business. This was her second visit to the law office, and she was confident it would be her last.

Tillie had asked Frank Smith of Howard and Smith Law Firm to draw up a durable power of attorney with Kathleen Larson as the principal and Tillie as the sole agent. It would give Tillie total control of finances, medical decisions, sale of assets, bank accounts, stocks and bonds, and insurance. In essence, this one document turned Kathleen's life over to Tillie Larson. If Kathleen signed such a document, she would be owned by Tillie, a condition that had been considered and rejected by Kathleen for years.

"My mother-in-law is in the early stages of Alzheimer's disease," she lied to the attorney sitting across from her. "I'm the sole caregiver since my husband died." She didn't tell him that her husband had died five years ago. "I've been forced to cut back on my work to care for Mom. If I'm going to be able to continue my work with the insurance company, I'll need some help. Mom has asked me to help her with her checkbook and to pay the monthly bills. She has really made a mess of the checkbook. Last week she asked me if I would straighten it out and I told her I would. Now she understands what I tell her, but in a few months or a year she might not be capable of making decisions."

"I can understand your need for power of attorney if you are the sole caregiver," said Frank.

"What concerns me the most is that several times she has gone for a walk, and has forgotten how to get back to the house," she was making it all up and he was buying it. "Thank God, most people in the neighborhood know her and have been able to help her find her way home. It really is amazing that some days she is perfectly lucid and on other days she doesn't know where she lives. Time sometimes doesn't mean anything to her. I'm concerned she'll go out during the night."

Tillie requested that Frank put all the legal information on the first five pages and save the last page for signatures. He didn't suspect foul play, but guessed that Tillie desired neatness. The only writing on page six was a place for Kathleen Larson's signature, Tillie Larson as the witness, and a notary public seal and the date. Tillie figured she'd have Kathleen sign the paper, telling her she was signing something else.

When she left the law office, she was pleased that step two of her plan had been accomplished. She would drop by her mother-in-law's house with a store-bought coffee cake and she resolved to be more solicitous than she had been in the past. She was certain the coffee cake would be appreciated.

At five-thirty, Tillie rang the doorbell and was received by a, "And to what do I owe this visit?" Kathleen was surprised to see her.

"I saw the coffee cake in the grocery store and thought of you. I know you like them, so I couldn't resist," Tillie said with a phony grin.

"I'm glad you couldn't resist. I'll put it in the refrigerator. My breakfast in the morning will be cake and coffee."

Kathleen still had her cast on but could hobble around the house without her walker when she wanted to. She took the cake and put it in the refrigerator, then returned to the living room and sat in her chair.

"Do you want a cup of tea, Tillie?"

"No, I've got to get home. I need to do some shopping and the cat needs to be fed. I just wanted to drop off the cake before I decided I needed it for breakfast."

"You're welcome to half," offered Kathleen.

"No, thanks. That's yours. I'll see you in a few days. Enjoy."

With that brief visit, Tillie was gone; leaving Kathleen to wonder what she was planning. *She always comes with a purpose,* Kathleen thought. *I can't remember another time when she just brought over a coffee cake for no reason.* No, Tillie was up to something. Kathleen was mystified but knew it must be a long-range plan. Only when all the pieces were in place would she understand the mystery. What she *was* certain of, however, was that her daughter-in-law could not be trusted.

Tillie stopped off at an office supply store during her lunch hour the following day. She searched and found legal documents already drawn up, just waiting for the signatures. There were boilerplate documents for selling a car, renting an apartment, Do Not Resuscitate forms, and forms for creating one's last will and testament. Finally, she found one document that gave permission to release medical information. It was perfect. It was only two pages long plus a third page for signatures. The type was a different font, but not so different that anyone would notice, especially since it was on a different page. Tillie was certain Kathleen wouldn't notice anything as insignificant as that.

What did concern Tillie was that the lawyer's signature page was numbered '6.' She knew tampering on her part could cause suspicion by any official who might view the document. Even King would be reluctant to accept it. So, Tillie spoke with several older secretaries and asked them how they fixed mistakes. One woman suggested she use white tape. White tape was the go to years ago, when secretaries used typewriters for all documents.

Tillie found a typewriter and some white tape in her office's supply room and brought them home to experiment. She typed out the number '3' on the white tape and taped it over a piece of paper. With the corner of a razor blade, she would be able to remove the tape, something she'd do after she retrieved the signatures.

Her correction was almost undetectable to the naked eye.

Back at her office, Tillie filled in the blanks on the store-bought document with her name and that of her mother-in-law. The document authorized Tillie to request and receive medical information should Kathleen be admitted to a hospital. It said nothing about Tillie having permission to make decisions with regard to the patient. The form seemed reasonable enough and was in clear, understandable language.

Tillie put the documents in her briefcase, hiding the durable power of attorney in a separate compartment. Her plan was moving forward according to schedule and she was pleased. She could hardly contain her pleasure with the brilliance of her plan. Perhaps she could get Kathleen to sign the form this weekend while they watched football. Everything was falling in line for her to take over Kathleen's assets. She just needed her mother-in-law to sign and her colleague to notarize. She was certain both would behave as expected.

CHAPTER TWELVE

Tillie didn't see an opportunity to broach the subject during the weekend. She told herself over and over that she needed to be patient or she would ruin her entire plan. She also found out that Kathleen was going to the doctor's office that week and they would probably remove the cast. Tillie decided to wait a few more days for the right moment to present her plan.

Kathleen couldn't drive with a cast on her leg, so she called the Senior Center and arranged for them to take her to the doctor's office at Brookwood Hospital. Due to her work hours, she didn't get to visit the center as much as she liked, but she was glad for their help now. Unfortunately, she had to call Tillie to pick her up after the appointment, as the center's van wasn't available at that time. And she wasn't happy about it.

When Tillie arrived, about an hour later, she first stopped at the administration office. She wanted to tell Kathleen how stingy they were about giving out information. It was all part of her plan.

"How did it go?" Tillie asked when they were in the car.

"They took the cast off and told me my leg was as good as new," Kathleen replied.

"What? No therapy?" Tillie asked as she turned the key in the ignition.

"They told me to walk each day, gradually increasing the distance. They told me not to push it, but to do some walking daily."

"I'm surprised they don't want you back for therapy."

"Oh, and the doctor told me I could drive the car. I feel like I'm almost back to my old self," Kathleen said with a smile and sigh of relief.

When they pulled into Kathleen's driveway, Tillie seemed anxious to leave. "Mom, I have to get back to work. Talk to you in a few days."

"Sure, Tillie." Kathleen said, concealing an eye roll.

She thought it strange that Tillie wasn't as pleased as she was about the cast being removed. Kathleen expected at least a little enthusiasm. But then again, it *was* Tillie. *How rude,* she thought.

Kathleen called Carol and left a voicemail explaining that her cast was removed, she was walking, and was given permission to drive again.

She then hurried to the grocery store, relieved to have freedom. People brought her the necessities, but there were things she needed to buy that she didn't want to ask others for. She needed toilet paper, olive oil, and fruit. Fruit was an item you had to pick out yourself, otherwise it could be too ripe or you might be forced to wait a week until it was ripe. She liked a certain brand of olive oil and didn't want to burden a neighbor to get the right bottle. And toilet paper? Well that was a personal matter. Just walking through the store was a treat after being locked up in the house for six weeks. She didn't realize how much she valued her mobility and independence.

When she returned back to the house, she saw Drew's car parked in front.

"Been waiting long?" she asked.

"No…probably five minutes. I knew you wouldn't be gone long when I saw the Buick was missing. I didn't know you were out of your cast."

Drew helped her bring in the groceries. Kathleen invited him to stay and enjoy tea with her and he did. He'd stopped by to tell her everything was settled. Any medical bills would be sent to the insurance company, and if her leg gave her any trouble, she was to contact the insurance company. He gave her a card with the name and phone number for Mr. Walter Wilson, the driver's insurance representative. He also handed her a check for $70,000.

"Drew, I don't know how to thank you. I didn't expect anything, and you have enriched my bank account by a great deal," Kathleen said with a chuckle. "I'll mail the check to my Vanguard account so Tillie won't know anything about it. She's a nosy one."

"Is she still trying to get you to turn everything over to her?" asked Drew.

"She hasn't said anything recently, but she'll be bugging me if I get sick or have an accident. You can count on that," Kathleen said, shaking her head. "For now, she's just trying to be nice to me. For her that isn't too easy. She'll start asking when I'll get the money from the insurance company. She'll want to know how much I've got and I don't intend to tell her. I don't think she likes me—and I don't like her. It feels like we're playing games."

"I'm glad you see that." Drew nodded. "I don't know her, but I would have to trust someone with my life if I was to give them durable power of attorney. Your child or husband might qualify, but not too many others. Maybe Carol would be the exception. She's a nice lady."

"I would trust Carol, although I know Tillie would blow a gasket if I gave her power of attorney. For now, I'm glad I don't have to make that decision."

"If Carol's not available, you can also set up a durable power of attorney with our law firm. You might consider me and another attorney as the agents. I think Carol is your best bet for now, but know we're available if you need us. Having a law firm handle matters like this is an expensive way to go, but better than having Tillie handle it. Consider Carol," Drew offered.

When he finished his tea, he hugged Kathleen and left. She knew he would have made his mother proud. *He's a nice young man,* she thought.

CHAPTER THIRTEEN

K athleen was putting the last few decorations on her artificial Christmas tree when the doorbell rang. Tillie had dropped in for a friendly visit. She rang the bell, but didn't wait for Kathleen to open the door. Finding it unlocked, she barged in.

"You should keep your door locked," Tillie said. "Anyone could just come in and take whatever they wanted."

It was the Saturday before Christmas. Tillie gave Kathleen a gift that was nicely wrapped and strictly admonished her not to open it until Christmas. Kathleen confessed that she hadn't done her Christmas shopping yet, but hoped to get to it this week.

"I wanted to tell you about something that happened at the hospital the other day," Tillie began. "When I came to pick you up, I asked the nurse to tell me how you were doing. She wanted to know who I was and why I was asking questions. Then she decided she wouldn't tell me anything anyway. She said just because we had the same last name, didn't mean we were related. She said she would let you tell me." All this nonsense was a big lie, but it supported Tillie's larger plan.

"Now, that's stupid," said Kathleen. "They don't seem to know when to give out information and when not to. That's really stupid." Kathleen wasn't sure she was buying what Tillie was selling, but she'd play along for now.

"I think I solved that problem," Tillie said with a sly grin. "I found a legal document at the office store that says I have permission to know your physical state—since I am your daughter-in-law, after all. It doesn't give me any other rights, only the rights to your current medical information."

"I don't see why that's even necessary," said Kathleen, still a bit skeptical.

"I don't either. Yet if any hospital insists on withholding information down the line, I'll be able to go around them. I'd keep the document in my car, just in case."

"Before I sign any document, I want to read it."

"Of course. Let me get it. It's in the car." Tillie bit her lip, wanting to squeal.

She didn't wait but shuffled off to her car without stopping to put on her coat. She returned in less than thirty seconds, shivering, and removed the document from a brown envelope. She handed all three pages to Kathleen who was still suspicious of Tillie's behavior.

Kathleen carefully studied the document. After several minutes, she flipped to page two and saw it was written in the same simple, straightforward language.

She looked for a loophole, but couldn't find any. Tillie remained quiet all the time Kathleen was reading.

Finally, Kathleen said, "Where do I sign?"

Tillie sprung to life. "Sign where the 'X' is and I'll sign below it. Don't worry, I'll fill in the date."

"What about the second witness and notary?"

"Don't worry about that. I'll have the notary be the witness. She'll take care of everything." She didn't want to answer any more questions and was anxious to leave as soon as possible. She ignored Kathleen's suggestion for a notary. "Listen, I've got to run. This will give me peace of mind should you ever end up in the hospital again." Kathleen shook her head. Sometimes it wasn't worth the effort to argue with Tillie.

When Tillie had the document secured in the brown envelope and tucked under her coat on the couch, she changed the subject to what they'd each be doing for Christmas. Tillie was going to visit her son in Atlanta and would be gone from Christmas Eve to the day after Christmas. Kathleen's granddaughter, Patti, was going to stop by on Christmas Eve with her husband and daughter, and Kathleen's son, Paul, would stop by with his wife and children on Christmas morning and stay for dinner. Kathleen wasn't a great cook, but Paul's wife, Nancy, insisted she would bring turkey, stuffing, and cranberries if Kathleen would do the carrots and potatoes. Kathleen felt she had the 'easy job;' it would be impossible to mess up such an easy assignment.

Tillie stayed just long enough so it wouldn't appear as if she were rushing to take care of business. She just couldn't wait to get out of the house, concerned she might reveal her pleasure with receiving the signature. Besides, she needed to get to her girlfriend's house so she could notarize the document and attest to seeing it signed. She was certain Janice would sign without a moment's hesitation and not ask any questions. That would make her rich.

At Janice Hoffman's house, Tillie heard her friend vacuuming, getting the house ready for company. She had to ring the doorbell several times before she heard the vacuum turn off. Janice knew she could go to jail if she notarized the document and it was later discovered she didn't witness the signature. She didn't hesitate, however, never even looking at it. She took out her seal and made the all-important impression on the document.

"Thanks, Janice," said Tillie. "I'd like to stay and talk but I have to run. See you at work."

"No problem," said Janice, without a moment's hesitation.

Once home, Tillie threw the store-bought document away. Carefully, using the corner of a razor blade, she removed the white tape with the number '3' on it. She returned the six pages of the durable power of attorney to her briefcase and let out a sigh. She'd make copies after the holidays.

CHAPTER FOURTEEN

The holidays were a happy time for Kathleen. In spite of her accident, this had been a good year. She had lost a few pounds and was feeling good. She attributed that to making simple meals, getting daily exercise, and limiting the size of her portions. Her relationship with her grandchildren was not as good or the visits as frequent as she would have liked, but pleasant when they got together. She always had a good relationship with Carol and that hadn't changed. If only Tillie wasn't so damn pushy and a 'know-it-all.' She secretly harbored the thought that she wished Tillie was out of her life.

Carol came over with her boyfriend, Rudy, to celebrate the arrival of the New Year. Carol was a diabetic and was advised to avoid alcohol. That was something her husband didn't do. Carol knew Kathleen had been 'on the wagon,' too, since shortly after her husband, Joseph died. His death had triggered some binge drinking that almost killed her, and now Kathleen vowed to avoid the booze. And she did.

Everyone thought it was a credit to Kathleen's will power that she was able to get off the stuff so easily. She knew spending New Year's Eve with Carol was safe. Rudy liked Kathleen, too.

"Turn on the show in Times Square. That's always the best," said Rudy.

"Rudy, what can I get you to drink? Orange juice, tomato juice, or a soft drink?" asked Kathleen. Rudy had been sober for about twenty years and seemed to have his drinking under control. He always enjoyed Kathleen's company.

"I'll have some OJ, with just a few pieces of ice. Thanks."

When everyone had a drink, the potato chips and dip were put on the coffee table where all could reach them. Kathleen had made some sandwiches of cream cheese and olives, cut off the crust and cut the bread into one inch squares. These were a big hit as she knew they would be. She also prepped some cheddar and Swiss cheese squares to go with crackers. Everyone brought their appetite. The three spoke of the past year and what was best. There seemed to be little concern about the coming year.

It wasn't the most exciting party on the street, but they didn't expect it would be. They all kissed when the ball dropped, Rudy and Carol spending enough time face to face to draw a comment from Kathleen.

"If you're gonna continue that lovey-dovey stuff, I'll just have to go outside and get me somebody."

"You probably could. Sorry Kay, the devil made me do it," laughed Rudy.

"You're forgiven. It's my daughter-in-law who's the naughty one," she insisted.

"Kay, look at him. Who can resist him?" Carol's comment was especially funny since Rudy was anything but handsome.

"Let me finish this sandwich and we'll be on our way," said Rudy.

School was back in session the following week and Kathleen spoke with the principal and told her she wasn't ready to return. The principal suggested Kathleen speak with the people at the school board as to her options. Ellen Goodwin in personnel reviewed for Kathleen the benefits she could expect should she wish to retire. Kathleen was concerned with what she should do about major medical since she was getting some benefits now because of the accident. Ellen said she would check it out and get back with her.

Kathleen gave it quite a bit of thought that week as she walked farther and farther each day in an effort to strengthen her leg. She came to the conclusion that she didn't need the money the job provided her and preferred to spend the time in the fresh air, at the Senior Center, visiting friends, playing cards, and reading rather than helping children cross the street. It was time for someone else to do that. After all, she was sixty-seven and soon to be sixty-eight.

The next day she drove to the Social Security Office to make arrangements. She wanted the money sent to her bank rather than directly to her. The young lady who waited on her was concerned whether Kathleen's leg would cause her trouble in the future and if she should apply for disability. Kathleen told her she didn't believe she would be disabled and that it was simply time for her to retire. She was pleased with herself for handling this chore.

CHAPTER FIFTEEN

*A*t nine on a crisp Monday morning, early in January, Kathleen left her house to walk to Patriot Park and the Senior Center. It was about half a mile and was the perfect distance for exercise. When she reached the park by way of Raleigh Avenue, she sat on one of the benches for five minutes. She didn't want to overdue the exercise and her leg was telling her that she had walked enough for the moment.

As she sat on the bench, she thought how nice it would be when her leg would be totally healed and she wouldn't have to worry about the distance she could walk. *I'll be able to walk to the park and several times around the track before I get worn out. When the weather gets better, I'll be the first one out here getting in shape.*

Kathleen looked forward to her visits to the Senior Center. She played canasta on Tuesdays and did floor exercises with a group on Wednesday in addition to her standing bridge appointment. When she had nothing to do and the weather was nice, she walked to the trail in

Patriot Park and went once around the track. Often, she would walk with another member from the center. If nothing was going on, she'd head back home.

She was surprised at how much she enjoyed these first days of retirement more than she had imagined. She was a people person and loved the chance to spend time with others. She attended lectures on health and listened to any special speakers who came to the center. She got to know quite a few members and enjoyed talking with them about their family or old times.

Talking with several of those she met, she found out a bus would take them to Philadelphia, Mississippi and they could spend a day gambling. She decided this might be a fun way to spend the day and told the staff at the desk to let her know when the next scheduled trip would take place. She learned that lots of trips were planned to various venues in the area. Some were even out of state. Overnight trips were advertised well in advance. She could hardly wait for the next trip to Branson, Missouri. All of this appealed to her and she wondered why she didn't know about these activities sooner.

For a nominal fee, she got lunch every day. It was amazing how much she could eat for such a small amount of money. She never finished what was put on her plate. Plus, with all the activity she felt she had even shed a few pounds. When she stepped on the scale at home, she found out she wasn't mistaken. She was extremely pleased with herself.

"Hey, Kay, do you want to use the machines in the weight room?" her friend Nancy asked.

"I wouldn't know where to begin or how to use them. I'm afraid I would hurt myself," Kathleen said, biting her lip.

"Tell the front desk you need a lesson and someone will help you get started."

Kathleen was put on the list for training—something she'd never imagined she'd try in the past.

CHAPTER SIXTEEN

*T*illie called the following Monday morning about eight-thirty. "Mom, I have to drive down to a facility that we insure in Shelby County. Since we don't get many nice days in January, I thought you might want to go for a drive. Maybe get out of the house. Since I'm only going to be but a few minutes at the facility, I thought you might want to join. I'm planning on stopping for lunch on the way home. Interested?"

"That would be nice, Tillie. How should I dress?"

"No need to get dressed up. Slacks and a blouse will be fine, although you might want to wear a sweater."

"When will you pick me up?" Kathleen asked.

"How does ten sound? Can you be ready by then?"

"Are you kidding? I'm ready now." Despite not being Tillie's biggest fan, it would be nice to go for a ride, she thought.

"Okay. See you at ten."

Kathleen didn't know what to make of Tillie's invitation. *Tillie has never invited me to go for a ride with her. Maybe she wants to bring up the durable power of attorney situation and wants me to be a captive audience,* Kathleen worried. *Riding in a car is about as captive as I can get. I'll find out what she has up her sleeve. No matter what's being planned, the answer will be 'no.' Tillie is not to be trusted.*

Tillie arrived about two minutes before ten and Kathleen was ready. She knew her chauffeur would be on time, as she always was. Kathleen closed and locked the front door, but didn't set the dead bolt. Tillie held open the passenger door for her mother-in-law; a suspicious act as far as Kathleen was concerned. Then she backed out of the driveway. Within several minutes they were driving south over Shades Mountain on I-65.

The ride was pleasant and Kathleen was surprised that nothing of import was brought up. When she asked where they were going, she was told it was out in the country. Tillie didn't have her GPS on since she knew the roads she would take and didn't want Kathleen to know where they were headed. Instead, she kept up a stream of conversation about the weather and the nice fields and how handsome the horses were in the pasture 'over there on the right.'

About forty minutes later they turned onto a narrow macadam road that led them through a heavily wooded area, mostly pine. An old sign, in need of paint, revealed they were at Lakeview Nursing Home. Kathleen commented she was surprised by how hidden the home was.

Tillie said Kathleen could go with her as she only had to drop off a document to Dr. King. Kathleen suspected nothing and took her purse with her, as was her habit. She commented on the size and shape of the big front door. "It looks like it was removed from Dracula's castle," she said. Both ladies chuckled. They waited at the front door and eventually heard the key turn in the lock.

Tillie spoke to the large woman in a white nurse's uniform. "Tillie Larson to see Dr. King."

"Let me escort you," the nurse said, then turned to Kathleen. "You go with these two ladies," she added, indicating the two women in pink uniforms who were waiting just inside the door.

"Give me your purse," Tillie said, as she snatched it from Kathleen's grip.

"Tillie, I don't want to go with these women. I'm staying with you." Kathleen could smell disinfectant and saw pitiful old men and women sitting at tables in the common room. She was *growing* more and more suspicious. One of the women in pink, probably twice the weight and at least a foot taller than Kathleen, took her firmly by the arm and led her toward a long corridor off the central room. The second woman took her other arm. Together, they dragged Kathleen who winced as her weight fell onto her bad leg. Another woman in white scrubs was waiting down the hall with one arm behind her back. As the three passed, she came up behind Kathleen and jabbed a needle into her left shoulder. Kathleen could feel the cold medicine squirting into the muscle, but didn't have time to scream. Within seconds she began to feel weak and in another brief moment, she lost consciousness. Tillie walked to the director's office to deliver him a copy of the fraudulent durable power of attorney.

"I have a *suggestion*, Dr. King," Tillie said with an inflection that implied 'suggestion' meant 'demand.' "List my mother-in-law as 'Helen Parsons' and put her on your roster with that name. I believe in several days people will be inquiring about any new additions to your patient list and it might be best if the name 'Kathleen Larson' didn't appear, understood? After a while, I figure no one will inquire anymore. You have a copy of the power of attorney. Hide it for now and in several months, you can put it in her folder. I'll send you half her social security every month. If you need to reach me, for any reason, please call me at the office."

"I will, Mrs. Larson. Don't worry. We'll take good care of your mother-in-law," King said as he rose from his chair and led Tillie to the door. "It's nice doing business with you."

CHAPTER SEVENTEEN

Kathleen awoke to gentle snoring sounds in the bed next to her. There was a window between the two beds and she could tell it was night as moonlight was making shadows on the floor from the bars on the window. She didn't want to move; her brain felt like jelly. She knew she would have to leave the bed as her bladder needed to be emptied, but she wasn't certain her rubber legs would hold her. She sat on the side of the bed and moved her legs in a circle, attempting to restore circulation. She needed to use the bathroom, *now*. Five minutes from now would be too late.

The bathroom door was just inside the door to the bedroom. She turned on the light and felt blinding pain in her eyes. She closed them and held on to the sink until she was acclimated to the searing illumination. Eventually, she took care of business. She wished she had a toothbrush. Using the wall as a prop to keep her upright, she turned out the light and returned to her bed, still dressed in the slacks and blouse she had put on this morning. She believed it was the same day, but was not at all certain. The lady in the next bed remained asleep.

Lying in bed, Kathleen watched the moon move into the trees and eventually disappear. *I haven't eaten all day and I'd give a month's salary for a bowl of cereal. What the hell happened to me? Did Tillie put me in a nursing home for crazy people? I think so. I knew she was not to be trusted. Damn. Damn! Did Tillie arrange for me to be held here against my will? How long will I be here?*

Hundreds of questions without answers left Kathleen reeling. She did not want to believe her own daughter-in-law would actually do something as evil as putting her in a nursing home against her wishes. Not only that, but a home inhabited by people who didn't have full use of their faculties. She'd seen the masses of old folks who shuffled about in the common room—not a one of them seemed to have their wits about them. Sometime before the sun rose in the morning, she fell asleep either from anger, or exhaustion, or both.

A loud alarm woke her the next morning. It could have been a fire drill since the noise sounded like the fire alarm they had at Hall Kent School. She heard her roommate puttering around behind her bed curtain and decided she would follow her when she left. In several minutes, she heard the curtain pulled back. She followed the tall, thin woman, her new roommate, down the hall to the big room.

Kathleen noticed her room was the last room on the right when headed away from the common room. In the common room, she counted twenty round tables with four chairs at most of them. Some tables had three chairs, leaving room to accommodate wheelchair patients. Staff members wheeled those who needed help to empty spots. Kathleen stood inside the common room, waiting to see if there was a chair for her. Everyone seemed wrapped up in their own thoughts and some could be heard murmuring to themselves as they shuffled about with walkers. No one was greeting anyone else, nor paying the slightest attention to her. As carts were wheeled out with food already on plates, Kathleen made her way toward an empty chair nearest her corridor. Her roommate was already seated at that table.

Her roommate was a pretty lady, tall and stately. She shuffled like all the others, but seemed to have some knowledge of who she was and what she was doing.

Breakfast was grits, a strip of bacon, an overcooked soft-boiled egg, and a piece of toast. No jam was visible for the toast, but small plastic cups of butter sat in the middle of the table. Workers dressed in pink placed cups on the table and poured coffee. Even with a cup filled to the brim, Kathleen could see the bottom. The coffee was as weak as chamomile tea. A half-pint milk carton and a plastic container of sugar were left on the table. Still, no one acknowledged her presence.

While sitting at the table, she could see four corridors. Each looked like they housed patients. She saw five rooms on each side of the hall and surmised that each room had two beds. She figured twenty patients could be housed in each wing, making total capacity about eighty patients.

Directly opposite the main entrance was a wall with a big mirror window. Kathleen suspected it was a two-way mirror. The staff could see in while no one could see out. She suspected if it was dark in the common room and lights were on behind them, she would be able to see what was behind the mirror. She figured that's where the administration offices were.

On each side of the huge mirror were locked doors that were opened by keypads. The nurses dressed in white scrubs and those in pink scrubs always used the door on the right. The kitchen staff and those in blue scrubs used the other door. Those who worked in the kitchen were dressed in green.

Two people in green scrubs pushed the food carts when food was being brought out or dishes taken back to be washed. It didn't appear as if any of the staff had much personal contact with the patients.

Kathleen didn't see any of the workers in blue, but she suspected they were cleaning people and would eventually arrive to go about their business. Those in pink pushed wheelchairs to tables that had empty spots. Then they would go down the corridor and come back with more patients in wheelchairs.

Most patients were women, though Kathleen counted about ten men as she looked around the room. The average age seemed to be about sixty, or at most seventy. She heard very few conversations, although there was some talking, for the most part by patients talking to themselves. As she was finishing up the two pieces of toast and had not as yet touched the cold grits, a staff member dressed in pink, came over and tapped her on the shoulder.

"Follow me," she said in a gruff, demanding tone. "Your presence is requested in the administration wing."

Kathleen followed past the tables to the administration wing. She was admitted through the door after the attendant pressed some numbers on the keypad. Halfway down the hall was a door on the right where she was directed and found herself standing before a man behind a desk. The wooden sign on his desk said, ALEX KING PHD, all in capital letters. The man behind the desk did not tell her to take a seat, nor did the petite staff member who stood behind her.

Dr. King was a big man. He was overweight by about thirty pounds, making him seem even larger. He was balding and the first signs of gray hair were showing amidst the hair that remained. Kathleen's first impression was that he was lazy, as was evidenced by his messy desk and wrinkled white coat. She felt this man was not to be trusted, even though he had yet to acknowledge her. She didn't have long to wait to find she was correct in her estimation.

"Mrs. Larson," he said sternly. "You will be staying with us for an extended period of time for observation. Your clothes and personal items will arrive soon and there is a chest of drawers and foot locker in your room for your clothes and personal belongings. There's a tall locker for your coat and bathrobe and the bag inside it is for laundry. The bathroom you will share with your roommate, Mrs. Whiteman; though she prefers her first name, Paige. Do you have any questions?"

"Yes," Kathleen said, wanting to shout. "Who said you could keep me here against my will?"

"Why you did, Mrs. Larson. You did that when you signed over durable power of attorney to your daughter-in-law. You gave her permission to do what was in your best interest and she did exactly that. It's our job to take care of you since you are no longer able to care for yourself."

"I can take care of myself!" Kathleen insisted. "And I never signed a durable power of attorney document. You must be mistaken."

"I'm afraid not," said Dr. King, holding up a document and flipping to the last page. "You signed right here, did you not?"

"I signed a document allowing her to see information from a hospital if I was hurt, not a power of attorney. That last page goes with a different document."

"You can say whatever you want, Mrs. Larson. You must be confused," he said, tapping the side of his head. "But I have a document that grants me the right to keep you at this facility until such time it is deemed in your best interest to be released. That decision will be made by your daughter-in-law."

"I'm not confused, damn it, and that's not acceptable. I wish to use a phone."

Both Dr. King and the staff member laughed. "I'm afraid we don't have phones for our patients," he said.

"This is the only phone." He gestured to the red phone on his desk. "And it's not for use by patients. And I'll give you one final word of advice: Don't make trouble or stir up the patients. Life can be uncomfortable when you're confined to small quarters and are not allowed to have three meals a day. You don't want to learn about that, believe me." Kathleen glared at him, dumbfounded. "Now, take her back to her breakfast," he added, gesturing toward the nurse in pink.

Everyone was finishing their meal when Kathleen was taken back to where she had been. She had not as yet finished her grits and wasn't sure she wanted to. She watched those in pink give pills to those who had finished their breakfast, followed by a glass of water. The nurses watched and waited until the pills were swallowed. She wondered if they'd know to give her the blood pressure medicine she took each morning.

CHAPTER EIGHTEEN

Tillie had Kathleen's purse. Her keys, credit cards, driver's license, social security card, and all kinds of medical information were included. She also had forty-three dollars in cash. Tillie spent the better part of the afternoon searching through these as well as several drawers at Kathleen's house. She was looking for documents and becoming well-acquainted with her new home. It wasn't hers yet, but would be one day...soon. For now, it was hers to use as she saw fit.

She found an accordion folder in the bottom drawer of a file cabinet with the last statement about Kathleen's mutual funds.

Look at this, Tillie thought. *That bitch has $41,000 plus in stocks and bonds. She also just deposited $67,000 to her money market account. That's what she got from the insurance settlement, I'll bet. Well, fancy that. We're rich, you old bitch. And you'll never get to use that money.*

Tillie was in a great mood. She also learned Kathleen had a safe deposit box at Regions Bank on Lakeshore

Highway and would receive a little over a thousand dollars in Social Security each month. She also owned a house, free and clear, and her Buick was free of debt. Tillie did a quick estimate of Kathleen's net worth and came to the conclusion it was over a quarter million dollars.

She estimated what she would have to send to Lakeside Nursing Home each month. Then she began an inventory of Kathleen's belongings, and before supper time, she listed all the items she wanted to get rid of. Of course, she'd move from her old apartment to her mother-in-law's house. It had more room and was much more comfortable.

But then Tillie had an even better idea. *If I sell this house and use the money to buy a condo, I can live very nicely with my present income and half of Kathleen's Social Security. And I won't have to be concerned about maintenance and upkeep. Maybe I'll start checking out a condo that will suit my needs.*

First among the items to sell would be the Buick. It was in good running condition, had very few miles on it, was only used around town and for church, and was well maintained. Then, she might be ready for an estate sale. Tillie could pay the neighbor boys to help her carry some of the furniture to sell.

The house phone rang, disturbing her planning. She dreaded the phone call, knowing sooner or later she would have to face Carol. Carol could cause trouble. Tillie decided to pick up the phone with, "Kathleen Larson residence." There was a short pause before Dr. King responded.

"Oh, hi, Dr. King," Tillie said. "How's my mother-in-law doing?"

"She's getting acclimated to her surroundings," he said, nonchalantly. "That will take a few days, usually a week or so. We need some clothes for her. Enough for about a week is all that's required. Several outfits with pants and blouses and dresses for everyday use, pajamas and a bathrobe, plus socks and underwear is all she'll need. We're not too big on social events around here," he said with a chuckle at the last part.

"I'll get them to you in the morning plus her toothbrush and shampoo. Maybe a few personal items. And I would prefer you not call me at this number. What if somebody else had answered?" she asked, thinking of Carol.

"I called the office and they told me you were sick today. I called your home number and finally found this number with Mrs. Laws...ahem...Mrs. *Parson*'s application. I thought it would be okay to call just this once since we have to get our stories straight and get Mrs. Parsons settled."

"I understand. Today was the exception." She was letting King know things would be done her way.

"Oh, when you come, come around the back and we'll take the items from you by the rear door. Better she doesn't see you. Also, tell me what medication she's taking or if you have her medication, please bring them. I can write prescriptions but it takes a few days or a week to fill them. The mail is reliable but slow and our prescriptions come from Canada. It would really help if you could come today. She needs a change of clothes."

"I'll be there tomorrow," Tillie said emphatically and hung up.

Tillie's brain was wrestling with a problem. She didn't doubt her ability to fool folks with the durable power of attorney document. It looked perfect. Nobody could guess it was obtained by fraud or that the notary hadn't actually witnessed Kathleen's signature. Tillie had made several copies in case they were needed, but if nobody requested a copy, she had no intention of giving them one. Since she removed the white out paper, the document looked perfectly legal. Everything appeared to be in order.

The following morning at work, Tillie stopped by her boss's office. "Anna Mae, I need to check on a nursing home that may be trying to cheat us. I'll be gone for about two hours."

"What's the problem?"

"Everything they send in is perfect. They never make a mistake and that's not the way most homes operate. I'd like to check on their personnel and why they feel the need to be perfect.

"You've been doing this a long time and I trust your instincts," Anna Mae said, barely looking up from her desk. "Tell me what you find. I'd be interested to know. See you this afternoon."

Tillie thought she might be back within two hours. As it was, she dropped off Kathleen's clothes and was back in the office within just over an hour. She told her boss she was mistaken; the nursing home in question kept accurate records because the clerk was obsessive compulsive and wouldn't allow herself to make a mistake. Tillie was "so pleased" to find out she was wrong. She never mentioned the name of the nursing home and got points for her thoroughness and ability to admit her mistake.

Tillie spent her lunch hour at the bank. She told the banker Kathleen Larson was in a nursing home and might be there for a while. She showed the banker the power of attorney document and he read it quickly.

"Janice Hoffman is a co-worker of mine and a notary." Tillie smiled.

"Let me get the forms for you to sign, Mrs. Larson, and you'll be able to assist your mother-in-law immediately. I hope she is well."

"Me, too. I know she appreciates having all these things taken care of. Having Alzheimer's just makes everything so much more difficult. When you get older, just paying the bills can be difficult, not to say anything about balancing the checkbook." After Tillie signed where the forms were marked with an 'X,' the banker made copies and gave them to Tillie. He didn't request a copy of the power of attorney. Tillie shook hands with the banker and left. A fast food burger helped her return to work before the lunch hour was up.

CHAPTER NINETEEN

The first day at the nursing home was the longest day Kathleen ever experienced. She was unable to talk with anyone since the other residents would only talk *at* her. Furthermore, no one made any sense. She heard nonsense and gibberish and crazy talk. It was as if nobody was 'home.' And when she finally found a person with a spark in their eyes that said they might have something understandable to say, she found within the first minute that she was mistaken.

She looked around at the common room and did not see anyone having a conversation. Some were talking, but they had no audience. Sometimes there would be four people at a table, nobody talking, just looking at the table or across the room. No one was playing cards or reading magazines or books. In fact, she didn't see any books or magazines or reading material of any kind. People were walking around, shuffling as they moved with no destination in mind and no discernible goals. There wasn't even a television set to relieve boredom or distract the patients.

At one table sat an old man in a wheelchair. He was speaking to a group that only he could see. He used his fingers to gesture and spoke to 'people' on his right, left, and directly across from him. Several moments later, he said goodbye and moved to another empty table to strike up another conversation.

A pretty lady who looked like she was about fifty shuffled from one person to another and pointed to her hair. She'd fluff her hair, nod to her friend, and continue on to show someone else.

Kathleen decided to check out what was in each corridor. In the corridor opposite her own, there were five rooms on each side and a window at the end of the corridor. Black bars graced the window, right to the top. Each room held two beds and a bathroom was behind each door. This corridor seemed to be an exact duplicate of hers.

As Kathleen made her way back toward the common room, a nurse dressed in a white uniform caught up to her.

"You're new here, so I don't expect you to know. Unless you are sick, or wish to use the bathroom or take a nap, you will remain in the common room. Do you understand?" the nurse asked, more telling than asking.

"Yes," said Kathleen with a sigh. "Where can I get something to read? A book or magazine?"

"People don't ask for those things here," the nurse almost laughed, notably surprised. But she recognized the authenticity of Kathleen's question and changed her tone. In a softer voice she added, "Maybe I can get you a paperback."

"I would appreciate it. Otherwise I'll go crazy," Kathleen said. *How prophetic,* she thought.

"I'll see what I can do," the nurse said, placing a hand on Kathleen's shoulder and gently nodding toward the common room. "Please go back to the common room."

After what seemed like an endless morning, a bell rang and the patients who were walking around gravitated to chairs at the various dining tables. There didn't appear to be any assigned seating, although some people had already claimed their spots. Kathleen waited until almost everyone was settled before looking for a seat. She found one next to her roommate, Paige. After a moment, the green-uniformed staff wheeled out carts and placed a plate in front of each resident. On each plate sat a chicken salad sandwich on white bread, a leaf of lettuce, a solitary slice of tomato, and a half dozen potato chips. Everyone received a half pint container of milk and a straw, and near the end of the lunch session, a nurse came by and placed three cookies on each resident's plate for dessert. No choices were provided and everyone got the same with no consideration for those who wanted more or couldn't eat what was presented to them. After about fifteen minutes had elapsed, the cafeteria workers began to pick up the plates and milk cartons, finished or not.

Kathleen asked, "Is this what it's like every day?" No one answered. She looked at her table mates and no one seemed inclined to provide eye contact. Finally, as she pushed her chair from the table, someone spoke.

"Sometimes the food is terrible. It was good today." The speaker was Paige Whiteman, her roommate. Paige spoke quietly, but refused to look up. Kathleen experienced her first glimmer of hope. *Is it possible I have found the one sane patient in this nursing home?* she thought. *Please, God. Let me be right.*

The afternoon was every bit as long as the morning. She wasn't used to inactivity unless she was watching television, and then at least her mind was engaged. There were some more comfortable chairs scattered about the perimeter and Kathleen noticed several couches with several groupings of chairs near the windows under the glass enclosed administration office. She counted, having nothing else to do, and found fifteen chairs along the wall. There were also two chairs between corridor A and B and between C and D. She thought these would have been taken first, but realized most were not used. It seems the patients preferred to walk or sit at the tables on hard chairs.

Kathleen found it strange that very few nurses or attendants were visible. She suspected the patients were being watched from behind the glass window in the administration offices. If two patients started to speak loudly or it looked like a scuffle was about to take place, one of the attendants would appear to separate the two. Most of the time it was those in pink scrubs who had contact with the patients.

There were two restrooms off the common room to the left and right of the big wooden entrance door. The smell of disinfectant was most noticeable near the restrooms. One was for the few men who lived in the facility and the larger room was for the women. There were hidden cameras in the women's restroom, though they weren't hidden *that* well as Kathleen spotted them almost immediately. She also noticed cameras spaced evenly in the common room, but not in the corridors. This allowed the staff to be as unobtrusive as possible.

By the end of the first day, it was obvious the purpose of this facility was to keep the patients fed and housed, and to see no one got hurt. It was a place where people who had dementia came to die. Or in her case, she was being sent to die even though she was sound of mind and body.

Supper was tomato soup, meatloaf, mashed potatoes, and string beans. Everyone attacked the soup first as if they knew it would be taken away if they didn't hurry up and drink it. It would not be considered hot but rather warm, bordering on lukewarm. While they were still on the soup, everyone received a plate with the main course. Then they were given their usual container of milk with a straw and the soup bowls were removed, finished or not. At Kathleen's table, everyone had finished. Since it was January, the sun set early and the flood lights in the ceiling were turned on. These were dimmed a bit after supper was finished.

Another hour passed with nothing to do, no one to speak with, no entertainment or news or stimulation of any kind. It struck Kathleen as odd that there was not a single television to be found. Then she noticed attendants coming out into the common room and, moments later, a bell rang. Thank God, it wasn't the same piercing bell that had woke her—that was, apparently, reserved for mornings. It was probably only seven o'clock, but she was unable to verify this since her watch had been taken from her when she was sleeping. All she remembered was the needle that was stuck in her shoulder and the dizziness and loss of consciousness that soon followed.

When the next bell sounded, everyone moved toward the corridors that housed the bedrooms. Kathleen welcomed the sound and was grateful this long day was finally over.

CHAPTER TWENTY

*C*arol hadn't heard from Kathleen for a few days. She and her mother-in-law would sometimes go three or four days between calls, but not usually. When Carol had called that morning, there was no answer. Even the voicemail didn't pick up and Carol thought that was strange. It wasn't like Kathleen to not let her know where she was. She decided to call back in a while.

All day, the results were the same. It was as if Kathleen had moved or was visiting relatives. Carol decided if she couldn't reach her by the evening, she would call Paul and Patti. Maybe they would know where she was. That evening when she called her children, they knew nothing. Both Paul and Patti asked if she had called Tillie to see if she knew anything. Carol said she would.

Tillie picked up on the second ring.

"Tillie, I've been calling Kathleen and she doesn't answer. Is something wrong?"

"I've been calling her, also," Tillie replied with her best air of faux-concern. "I meant to call and ask if you knew where she was. I assumed she was with you."

"She isn't," Carol said, feeling increasingly concerned. "I'm going over to her house to see if she answers or if the neighbors know anything. Please call me on my cell phone if you hear from her or get any information."

Carol hung up and called Rudy. "Hey Rudy, want to take a trip?"

"Not especially. What'cha got in mind?"

"I can't get Kathleen to answer her phone and Tillie claims she doesn't know where she is. Maybe Kay fell or is unconscious in the house. She could have fallen and broken a hip and maybe she can't move. I'd like to check. Would you pick me up?"

"See you in fifteen minutes," he said. Rudy was abrupt and could be as snotty as hell, but never failed to be there when you needed him. He had a heart of gold, but was the most negative person Carol knew. He talked rough, was rude, and sometimes didn't seem to give a damn, yet he would give you his wallet if you were short a few bucks. He was always there for Carol when she needed him.

Kathleen's house was dark when they arrived in her driveway. No lights were on inside or out. They peeked through the windows and saw nothing. The Buick was in the garage. Carol called on her cell, but received no answer. They thought it might be wise to stop by a neighbor's house to see if they knew anything. The neighbor said she hadn't seen Kathleen all day and could add nothing to what they already knew.

The neighbor on the other side of Kathleen's house had a bit more information. "I saw a Mustang in the driveway for a few minutes about mid-morning on Monday. I think Kathleen left the house and went for a ride in that car. It returned for a short while in the afternoon but I don't believe Kathleen was in the car. I believe it might have been her daughter-in-law; the car was new and black. I've seen no activity since and no lights have been turned on."

"It's time to call the police," said Rudy as they walked back to the house. "We need to get in and look around. She could be lying on the floor. Hold on," he said, reaching for his wallet. "This might work. I know she is in the habit of using the dead bolt on the door when she's home, but she only shuts the door when she leaves, automatically locking it. Maybe a credit card will get us in."

Rudy found a credit card in his wallet and inserted it into the space between the jam and the lock. Surprisingly, the door opened. "Some security system," Carol muttered.

"I'll wager ten to one she's not at home," said Rudy. "If she were, the dead bolt would be on." He turned a light on in the living room.

Carol called out Kathleen's name several times as she moved from the living room to the kitchen, then down the hall to the bedroom, turning on lights along the way. Her mother-in-law wasn't home. They continued searching until they were sure she wasn't there. They even searched the shed before Carol called the police.

The police arrived about twenty minutes later, took the necessary information, and asked the questions they needed to ask, but they mentioned it was not a missing person's case until forty-eight hours had elapsed. Carol told them it must be a kidnapping case since there was no way Kathleen would leave without telling someone. Besides, her car was still in the garage. Carol also told them she didn't believe Kathleen's daughter-in-law, Tillie, when she said she hadn't spoken with her. She gave the police Tillie's address and phone number.

Rudy listened carefully and determined she needed legal help. "I'm with you, Carol," he said. "I can't imagine she would give Tillie power of attorney, and Tillie would be the only person she would let take her somewhere. Call Drew. You need some legal advice."

After the police left, Carol called Drew, having kept the business card from when she arranged an attorney to help Kathleen. The voicemail picked up on the fourth ring and she was forced to leave a message. "Drew, this is Carol Larson. I believe Tillie may have kidnapped Kathleen. Tillie told me she hadn't seen or spoken with Kathleen, but I don't believe her. Kathleen is not in her home and her car is still here. Tillie is the only person she would go with. Call me on my cell, even if it's three in the morning." She hung up.

Drew called shortly after ten. Carol was back at her apartment and answered her cell. "Carol, this is Drew," he said. "Tell me what you know."

Carol told the story as she lived it and Drew wisely said this would best be solved in the morning. "We can't do anything tonight," he said. "I'll call you in the morning and we'll see what can be done. Don't worry, Carol. We'll find her and get this straightened out. I know she would never give Tillie power of attorney. She must have been tricked. See you in the morning."

CHAPTER TWENTY-ONE

*I*t was shortly after eight when Drew's Honda Accord pulled into Kathleen's driveway. Carol had asked him to meet her there as she knew where Kathleen kept her paperwork. Carol was dressed for work but had called her boss and told her she would be late, that she'd had an emergency. Drew joined her for a cup of coffee and expressed his deep concern for Kathleen.

"I talked to her about durable power of attorney and she told me she wouldn't give Tillie that power," he said, shaking his head. "If the time came when she had to, she said she would give it to you. She even asked if our firm could handle that and I told her we would be happy to take the responsibility, but it would be expensive. In any case, she had no intention of handing it over to Tillie."

"How do we find out if there is a power of attorney document?" asked Carol.

"Most people go after the easy things first, such as her checking account. Do you know where she banks?" Drew asked.

"Yes. Regions Bank on Lakeshore. I believe there is some information in her file cabinet," Carol said.

"Let's check that first," Drew said as he moved toward the cabinet. "I would also like to talk with the police and let them know we recently spoke about POA and she was considering you and our firm. I want them to know she's well represented and they can't just push this case under the rug."

"Thank you, Drew, for taking such an interest in Kathleen," Carol said, shaking his hand.

"I'm still her attorney and she's a sweet lady. My schedule is fairly light, so I don't mind. I'll see what I can do."

It was after lunch when Drew was finally free to inquire about Kathleen Larson's checking account. He had written the name and address of the bank and her account number in his notebook.

Drew drove to Lakeshore Highway and parked in the bank's parking lot. He looked around and found a cubicle with a sign that said, 'Manager: James Belcher.' The manager had someone with him, so Drew took a seat facing the office, hoping he wouldn't have to wait long.

When the manager was free, Drew walked toward his cubicle and was invited in. There were some preliminary introductions before Drew explained the reason for his visit.

"My name is Andrew Stephens, Mr. Belcher. I represent Kathleen Larson, most recently in an insurance case in which she won a fairly large sum of money. We believe one of her relatives wants her money and has somehow provided a durable power of attorney document to gain control of her assets. Tell me, has anyone taken control of Kathleen Larson's checking account?"

"Yes, Mr. Stephens," Belcher said. "In fact, Tillie Larson was just in the other day and showed us a power of attorney document, claiming Mrs. Larson could no longer take care of herself. She said she would pay her bills and see to her finances."

"May I see that document of durable power of attorney?" Drew said, somewhat suspicious.

"Oh, I didn't keep it," Belcher said with a wave of the hand. "I looked at it carefully and since it was notarized and everything seemed in order, I put Tillie Larson on as a co-signee. She can sign for Mrs. Larson. She's the legal custodian of those funds, according to the document she presented."

"Did you see the *original* document?" Drew pressed.

"Yes." Belcher paused. "It was the notary seal that convinced me it was real and I didn't pay too much attention to anything else. Do you believe it was forged?"

"I'm not sure it was forged, but I do know my client would never give her daughter-in-law power of attorney. She could have believed she was signing some other document. We discussed this the last time I saw her and who would be a good custodian. Our firm was considered. She didn't trust Tillie and wanted to be certain she couldn't get her hands on her insurance money, house, car, or stocks."

"You believe this woman is stealing from Mrs. Larson?" Belcher asked, growing increasingly concerned that he'd made a mistake not taking more care with the account.

"I'm afraid she has done that and maybe more. Mr. Belcher, I believe Tillie Larson has perpetrated a fraud and has kidnapped Kathleen Larson. Would you see that no funds are transferred out of her account until we get this matter settled? I'll get this authority from a judge. In the meantime, don't let the account be raided."

"I can hold the funds temporarily on a technicality until you bring me a court order. I'll just tell Mrs. Larson it takes time to make the necessary changes. She'll buy that."

"You're going to have to do better than that since we are dealing with a large amount of money here. You could be accused of not taking due diligence to make sure the document was genuine. Nor did you keep a copy of it. The bank could be held responsible." Drew said.

"I'll make certain no money is withdrawn from the account," Belcher said as he rose from his chair and offered Drew a hand to shake.

"Good. Please do," said Drew. "To arrest Tillie we'd need more information—like if Kathleen actually gave her the POA. We also need to locate Kathleen. She is missing and a check might tell us where she is being held. Here is my card. I can be reached anytime."

The two men shook hands and Drew left the building. He called Carol to update her and in particular mentioned the track he'd placed on Kathleen's check book.

Drew called his office to find out which judge should be called to place the freeze on Kathleen's account. He was new to the firm and wasn't sure he would get the consideration he needed if he chose the wrong judge. Besides, he was young and didn't know any of the judges or who would be the best choice for this problem.

He spoke with his boss, Jack Martin, who said, "Andrew, let me handle the judge. There are several with whom we have very strong relationships and they wouldn't know you. They would most likely deny your request. I'll handle it; this just eliminates the middle man. Give me a call in the morning and I'm certain I'll have the permission in writing by then."

CHAPTER TWENTY-TWO

*K*athleen woke to the sound of someone whispering 'Helen,' over and over in her ear. She finally emerged from sleep to find Paige Whiteman trying to get her attention. From the fact she couldn't see moonlight on the floor, she concluded it must be the middle of the night.

"Helen, I need to tell you something." Paige was dressed in a long, white sleeping gown and was standing less than a foot from her face. She was tall, slender, and spoke with a sweet voice.

"Okay. Give me a few seconds to find out where I am," said Kathleen.

"Take as long as you need. I have all night," Paige responded.

"Okay. What do I need to know?"

"You and I may be the only ones here who have our minds," Paige whispered. "It took me all day yesterday observing you to be sure. Most of the other patients are like zombies; they give us a pill each morning in our grits, but I noticed you didn't eat yours, because you were meeting with Doctor King. If you use your fork, you'll be able to locate it. It's white, just like the grits, but hard. Don't let them see you remove it or they'll mash it up. I put it on the side of the plate and then cover it with my thumb and slide it into my dress pocket."

"How did you know my name?" Kathleen asked suspiciously. She wasn't sure she could trust anybody at this place.

"I overheard one of the staff call you Helen. While we can be friends, it wouldn't be wise to be seen together during the day. They watch us, you know, behind that glass mirror in the administration office. I think they don't trust me because I do a poor job playing like I'm a zombie. By the way, my name is Paige."

"Nice to meet you, Paige," Kathleen said, as she propped herself up on one arm. "It's good to know there's another sane person here beside myself. My name is Kathleen Larson, not Helen."

"Oh," Paige sighed. "That must be the alias they're using if anyone inquires about Kathleen Larson. So, I guess if people ask about you, they can say you're not here."

"I'm sure that's what's happening," said Kathleen, rubbing her eyes.

"I'm glad we're roommates. We can talk at night and share experiences. How come you're in here when you don't need to be?" Paige asked. Kathleen could sense eagerness in her voice and figured it had been some time since she'd had a real conversation.

"My daughter-in-law has been trying to get durable power of attorney and I won't give it to her. I believe she forged a document and now I'm stuck here. What's your story?"

"My daughter does drugs. She arranged this whole situation, saying I was crazy. She hopped me up on pills and brought me here for 'evaluation.' She is the second signature on my banking account."

"Geez. Well, how can I tell someone where I am?" asked Kathleen.

"I don't know. I'm sure there's a phone in the administration wing. I once thought I heard a phone ring when the door opened. It was near Dr. King's office. When they took you to see him, did you see a phone?" Paige asked.

"I may have...but I don't remember," said Kathleen. Though she definitely didn't have Alzheimer's, her memory wasn't as sharp as it had once been. "Oh, yes—I remember! There was a red phone on his desk. When I asked to use it, they laughed. I was trying to figure out who was behind bringing me here but they said that phone is for staff only. Maybe one of the attendants has a cell phone. If only we could get our hands on one for five minutes, I could call the authorities and tell them where we are."

"Do you know the name of this place?" asked Paige.

"Yes. It's Lakeside Nursing Home. That's what the sign said, but I didn't see a lake," Kathleen said, rolling her eyes.

"Good. I was so drugged up, I didn't see the sign. Let's get some sleep and we can talk tomorrow night. Watch for the pill at breakfast," Paige added as she headed back to bed.

CHAPTER TWENTY-THREE

When Drew arrived at work, he found a judge's order sitting on his desk to temporarily freeze all of Kathleen Larson's assets until further notice. He immediately called the bank and advised James Belcher, letting him know he'd send a scanned copy ASAP. He then spent the better part of the morning calling nursing homes in Jefferson, Shelby, and St. Clair counties. He was quite certain Kathleen wouldn't be in a retirement home as they were not secure; people could phone out or walk out the front door. No, Kathleen would most likely be held at a place that housed patients. His bet was a nursing home and most likely one that housed Alzheimer's patients. For now, he decided to limit his search to facilities that were in state and within a hundred miles.

By about four in the afternoon and having made no progress in locating anybody by the name of "Kathleen Larson," Drew had begun to suspect that Tillie hadn't used Kathleen's real name, but had instead created an alias. He also suspected she might have some previous knowledge of the home, or was maybe friends with the administrator. With all the money she was planning to steal, there was no telling whom she could bribe. Drew also remembered how Tillie dealt with insurance and figured the nursing home could be a client. In fact, the more he thought of the possibility, the more plausible it sounded.

Drew stopped by his boss's office before going home. Jack Martin waved him in. "Andrew, did you get the judge's order?"

"Yes, and I called the bank. They're anxious to cooperate since I told them they could be held responsible for not taking due diligence in recognizing and obtaining a copy of the POA."

"You've done a good job on your first case, Drew," his boss said with a nod. "You're fast and professional and you did your client a favor. That was handled nicely. I hope this will work out for you as well. Did that court order settle everything?"

"I'm afraid this job isn't over. Because I got Mrs. Larson some money from the accident, she is now missing." Drew explained what had happened and that he suspected foul play. He told his boss he believed Tillie's power of attorney document to be forged, even if it *was* supposedly witnessed by a notary.

"Get a copy of the document and we'll be able to see if it's real or not," his boss said.

"I'll try, but that might be harder to do than one would believe. I was already late in stopping Tillie's ability to write checks, but I've put a temporary freeze on the account now. If I can get ahead of her next move, say trying to sell Kathleen's car or her house or maybe her mutual funds account, we can get a copy of the POA. I have some ideas. I tried to figure out if she's hidden away at a nursing home, but that turned out to be a waste of time. My next move will be to freeze her mutual funds. I'll keep you informed."

The phone rang on Jack Martin's desk providing Drew with the opportunity to leave.

When he reached his Honda, Drew called Carol and got her voicemail. He left a message saying he needed to talk with her and was on his way over. When he arrived at her apartment twenty minutes later, she had just arrived from work and hadn't even taken off her coat. They sat at the kitchen table and Drew brought her up to date.

"Tillie produced a power of attorney document to the bank. They believed it to be genuine but I told them it was false and we have a court order from a judge to keep Kathleen's assets frozen. That will give us some time," said Drew.

"Now what do we do? We have to find her." Carol insisted. "Did I mention that she has something to do with insuring nursing homes? We need to check them out."

"Don't worry, we will. I'll do that first thing in the morning. First of all, I want to beat Tillie to the punch. What do you think her next move will be?" Drew asked.

"If I were Tillie, I'd go after that Vanguard money," Carol said. "Kathleen sent it to her mutual fund account. All of it. There was also about forty thousand invested already. When Tillie gets Kathleen's mail and sees how much is in that account, she'll make a beeline to get it all before anyone suspects what she's doing. She may even have searched her house so maybe she already knows how much is in the account. Then maybe she'll put the house on the market or move into it. It'd be smart of her to just move in since it's all paid for, except for taxes," Carol wrung her hands as she considered the damage Tillie might do if not stopped.

"Tomorrow I'll talk with the mutual fund people and alert them to the possibility of fraud. I also believe Kathleen might be held in a nursing home under an assumed name. That makes sense to me since the home may have something to do with the insurance Tillie's company provides. She could know the director of a nursing home and might even have some influence over a director," Drew suggested.

"Drew, I like the way your mind works. I thought I could be devious, but I believe you could outfox me," Carol said with a smile on her face. "You're one devious son-of-a-bitch."

"I guess it takes one to know one. In any case, I'm going to take that as a compliment. Now we have some work to do. Do you have any suggestions?"

Between the two of them, they made a list of items to be done and questions to be answered. Drew drove home with an impressive list of to do items that would keep him busy for at least a day. He was concerned with what needed to be done first.

CHAPTER TWENTY-FOUR

athleen awoke to the disturbing screech of
the horn. *I'll never get used to that sound,* she
thought. When she opened her eyes, she saw a
woman in pink standing at the foot of her bed. When the
horn stopped its insane noise, the staff member spoke.

"I put clothes in your drawers. Someone brought
them for you. The bag hanging in the locker is for your
laundry. There is also a book one of the staff brought
for you. She said she doesn't need it back," her words
were emotionless, like a well-rehearsed speech given by
an eight-year-old. "Oh...and I have been given some
pills for high blood pressure you are to take every
morning after breakfast. I understand this is the only
medication you take?"

"That's all except for the occasional aspirin or Aleve
when my arthritis becomes too annoying," said Kathleen.

"Good. I'll be giving you that blood pressure pill
every morning," said the woman in pink who then
turned and abruptly left the room. Kathleen didn't even
have time to say 'thanks' for bringing the book.

Kathleen dressed and looked at the book. It was a Sue Grafton novel, *W is for Wasted*. She was familiar with Sue Grafton and looked forward to reading it. She tucked the book under her pillow then turned to her clothes.

Having lived in the same clothes for two days, she felt grungy. There was a shower stall in the bathroom, but the staff ran such a tight ship, she'd need to find out when she could use it.

Kathleen noticed staff members wore different colored uniforms. The nurses were in white, the assistant nurses in pink, those who worked in the kitchen or served food were in green, and the cleaning staff was in blue. Those who worked in administration wore street clothes.

When the staff member left, Kathleen closed the door.

"Good morning, Paige," she said quietly.

"Good morning, Kathleen. I'm glad you've been given some clothes."

"Me, too. I needed a change." She pulled the curtain around the bed after she selected a new pair of slacks, a tee shirt, and a blouse. "See you at breakfast. Oh, by the way, when can I take a shower?"

"After breakfast, ask one of the ladies in pink. They'll tell you when you can," said Paige.

"Thanks. I may take a while to learn the rules."

"Don't forget to find that pill," Paige warned. "Otherwise, in a few days, you'll be shuffling like everyone else. The pill takes a few days to really hit you, but you're going to have to learn to walk with a shuffling gait like everyone else or they'll become concerned you're not normal. They might believe the pill is not working and then they'll just give you a stronger pill."

"I will," Kathleen said, as she sat on the edge of the bed and put on her socks and shoes. Kathleen was glad her roommate was normal and not sick with dementia. Still, Paige had learned to keep to herself, take small steps, and shuffle like the others did. She even took to talking to herself. Paige was smart and Kathleen knew she would have to learn to act like her roommate. So for starters, Kathleen walked to the common room a bit more slowly than usual. She thought maybe it would be wise to read her book in bed at night. If she read it during the day in the common room, the staff would know the pill wasn't doing what it was supposed to do.

She found an empty seat and was served almost immediately by a young lady in green. The usual fare of grits, an egg, toast, and one strip of bacon was set in front of her as she fumbled for her fork and took a bite of the grits. When no staff member was around, she started to mash the grits and was rewarded almost immediately with the feeling of something hard. She pulled the pill to the side of the plate and covered it with the piece of toast. Moments later, she put her thumb over the white pill and slid it into her pocket. *Next time,* she thought, *I'll put some toilet paper in my pocket so I can throw the pill out more easily.* It might also be wise, she considered, to choose a seat so her back was facing the mirrored wall. She didn't know if she was being watched, but certainly didn't want anyone to see her dispose of the white pill. Still, she was quite confident no one could tell what she was doing.

When breakfast was over and people were moving around, she went to the bathroom and flushed the pill down the toilet. She cleaned her pocket as best she could, and put a piece of toilet paper in it for tomorrow. She didn't know what specific pill they were giving everyone, but she knew she should start acting lethargic. Everyone else seemed like they were in slow motion, which would require some serious acting skills like she saw Paige display. For today, she would slow up just a little.

CHAPTER TWENTY-FIVE

*D*rew was at his office at seven-thirty the next morning making out his 'to do' list. First on his list was a visit to the Homewood police to review his client's status and, now that 48 hours had passed, to make sure she was officially reported as 'missing' from her home.

As yet, the police had no clues but offered to send someone to talk with her neighbors.

"Do you know who else she may have contacted?" asked Officer Rogers, the same detective Carol had spoken with two days prior. He was scrounging for all the information he could get before he let Drew leave.

"I would check her daughter-in-law, Tillie Larson in Homewood and you have met Carol Larson, her first daughter-in-law who also lives in Homewood. Kathleen has never trusted Tillie but trusts Carol." Drew filled the police in on the freeze he'd placed on Kathleen's account and Tillie's obtaining a POA fraudulently. He'd need their help to prove it. "Something is not right and

I believe Tillie is behind it," he added, leaving Officer Rogers contact information for both Tillie and Carol.

When he hung up, he turned his attention to the mutual funds account. He'd had Carol pull some files at Kathleen's house that contained her account number and pertinent security information, like her social security number. It took more time than he anticipated to reach a broker who could help him, but eventually found the brokerage company willing to go out on a limb to protect one of their clients. They promised Drew no money would be dispersed from the account or any mutual funds traded until they were satisfied the durable power of attorney was authentic. They took down Drew's name, number, and information and told him they would make some inquiries to make sure he was who he said he was. They also requested Drew fax the court order from the judge. Drew was pleased they were taking the investigation so seriously.

Next, Drew called Carol to get information about where Tillie worked, what she did, and if she had any friends who might have information. Carol couldn't name any of her friends, but knew where Tillie worked. "And I got a call from the Homewood Police," said Carol, "asking me questions about Tillie. I presume you told them to call me."

"I did. You know much more about Tillie than I do. I hope they treat it as a missing person's case, or better yet, as a kidnapping."

"I'll call if I hear anything else," Carol said.

Drew said goodbye and immediately called the bank. He again spoke with Mr. Belcher and asked him to call Tillie Larson and tell her the bank needed a copy of the POA form. "Tell her it was your mistake and that since you are new to being a manager, you were new to handling those cases," said Drew. "Tell her your boss told you a copy of the document had to be in Kathleen's file." Drew suggested Belcher ask Tillie to send the document by courier to speed things along.

Next, Drew called the Homewood Police again. The receptionist transferred him to Officer Rogers. "What can you tell me, Officer? Should we be worried?" Drew asked.

"I think you have cause to be concerned," the officer sighed. "Both next door neighbors said it was not like Kathleen to leave without telling them to watch the house. She always keeps them informed even if she's going to be away for a short time. One neighbor said she thought a black Mustang was in her driveway the other morning. The same car that often visits."

"I understand Tillie has a black, late model Mustang. Everything keeps pointing to Tillie. My gut is telling me she's behind Kathleen's disappearance," said Drew.

"I got Tillie's work address from Carol," said Officer Rogers. "I'll take another officer with me and have a talk with her. Maybe we'll know more this afternoon."

"I'd appreciate a call when you know something," Drew said before he hung up.

CHAPTER TWENTY-SIX

*A*t the Acme Insurance Company office just off Lakeshore Parkway, Tillie was on the phone when the officers arrived. The detectives asked the receptionist to get her supervisor, if she would. The supervisor was a middle-aged woman, rather tall and slender by the name of Anna Mae Glass.

"What can I do for you, officers?" she asked.

"We would like to speak with Tillie Larson privately. We are trying to locate her mother-in-law who appears to be missing," said Officer Rogers.

"Susan, please call Tillie and tell her she has visitors," she said to the receptionist. She led the officers to a small conference room and indicated where they could sit around a table that would seat six.

Tillie entered several moments later and acted surprised when she saw the policemen. "Yes, officers, how can I help?"

"We are trying to locate Mrs. Kathleen Larson, your mother-in-law. Do you know where she is?" asked Officer

Rogers. He was the senior detective and was taking charge of the interview. His tone was not accusatory.

"No. I suspect she's at home," said Tillie, doing her best to play dumb.

"She isn't. When did you last see her?" Again, he was careful not to let his suspicions tip Tillie off.

"Oh dear. It was several days ago. I picked her up and brought her to this office to sign a power of attorney form and have it witnessed. Then I drove her home."

"Are you telling me she asked you to be her agent to handle all her affairs?" The officer asked, his voice slightly higher.

"Yes. She has been concerned ever since she had that accident at the school when she broke her leg. She felt like she needed help with the house and finances, especially after she received that nice insurance settlement," Tillie said, being careful to add, "I hope she's okay."

"And you asked her to sign a POA agreement?" the officer asked.

"Yes, that's the least I could do. I'm her nearest relative," Tillie said.

"And who witnessed the signature and had it notarized?"

Here, Tillie hesitated. "I'd rather not say."

"You do realize, Mrs. Larson, a notary is a state official in so far as that function is concerned. I need to know who the notary is and will need to speak with that person."

"Janice Hoffman is our notary. She witnessed my signature as well as Mrs. Larson's and then notarized it," Tillie lied.

"Is Janice Hoffman in the office today?" Again, she hesitated.

"I believe she is," Tillie said.

Officer Rogers asked the receptionist to call Janice Hoffman to the front. When Janice appeared, Tillie was dismissed. The officer didn't want the two women to synchronize their stories. He figured Janice might be intimidated by Tillie.

"Are you Janice Hoffman?" he began after they were seated in the conference room.

"Yes," she said, "How may I help you?"

"Are you a notary public?" he asked, cutting straight to the chase.

"Yes."

"How long have you been a notary?"

"Twelve years," Janice said, raising her brow in curiosity.

"Have you witnessed many signatures during your time as a notary?" The detective wanted to make sure she understood the gravity of her position.

"Yes, sir. The company has used me almost exclusively during my twelve years in this position," said Janice.

"Was Kathleen Larson in front of you when you notarized the document Tillie Larson brought before you?" Officer Rogers asked.

Janice knew this question was coming and wanted to lie. She also knew she could be put in jail for perjury if she did. There was a considerable pause before Janice finally said, "No."

"Thank you for your honesty, Ms. Hoffman. Please understand you will lose your status as a notary as a result of this confession," stated Officer Rogers. "I am pleased you are not going to add perjury to that charge. A policeman will take your statement. Please remain here."

It took just a minute for the other officer to record who was in front of him and that she had falsely notarized an official document that was presented to her at her home by Tillie Larson, a co-worker and friend. The officer also recorded other vital information, such as her address and driver's license number. Then, the policeman asked her to get her seal.

Finally, Officer Rogers asked the receptionist to call Tillie Larson to the conference room once more and to bring her coat. "We're bringing her downtown for questioning," he added, eyeing Anna Mae who's mouth fell open at his words.

Several moments passed and Officer Rogers was becoming uncomfortable. He was used to things happening when he expected them to happen and he believed he should not have been kept waiting so long. "Can someone take me back to where Mrs. Larson works?" he requested.

At that moment, the receptionist approached Anna Mae and spoke loud enough for everyone to hear.

"Mrs. Larson is not at her cubicle. Apparently, she said she was going out for a smoke immediately after she came back to her desk…but she doesn't smoke. She grabbed her coat went down the back stairs and hasn't come back. That was about fifteen minutes ago."

Officer Rogers asked the other officer with him to check if she was downstairs and if her car was in the parking lot. "It's a new black Mustang. You can't miss it."

CHAPTER TWENTY-SEVEN

*P*aige Whiteman had spent approximately two months in Lakeside Nursing Home. Yet she was still not certain if it was a day or two less than two months, or a day or two more. She had to keep track of the days of the week in her head, and not having a calendar made the task a bit confusing. She didn't get any clues from the staff since it appeared one day was exactly like the last. Nor would the next day be any different.

Paige used her understanding of how the home operated to avoid trouble and to keep from taking the dreaded white pill. And she used her intelligence to keep her sanity. That proved no easy task. She was only sixty-five years old, a vibrant woman with many years of life ahead of her. She considered herself fortunate her daughter could co-sign on her checks, but did not have power of attorney. Her daughter, Daphne, evidentially saw the checkbook was fat, five thousand dollars plus being 'fat' in her eyes, and calculated just how many drugs that would buy. She'd arranged to bring Paige to the nursing home, which she did with the help of a few pills, and let Dr. King take it from there.

How Paige's daughter had found out about this particular nursing home or that the director would assist her in this scheme, was a mystery to Paige. Every month, she deposited her mother's social security check in the checking account and sent the money to the nursing home. Paige was thankful her daughter couldn't get the real money, which was in stocks and bonds. Paige's home was worth half a million and was not available to her daughter. Besides, it was much too large for Paige and she planned to put it on the market when she got her freedom.

Paige was five-foot-six and had pure white hair. Kathleen admired her hair and slender figure. *She must have been a beauty when she was younger*, Kathleen thought.

Paige had checked the bedroom for listening devices and cameras several weeks ago and couldn't find any. She saw the camera over the door but knew it was useless when the room was dark and surmised it probably didn't work in the daytime, either. She wondered what this facility was before it was used as a nursing home. She guessed it had been a detention home of some sort, though she couldn't say for certain. She could not think of any reason why they would want to track patients in their bedrooms. After all, they all talked gibberish or didn't talk at all and there was no way to escape from the bedrooms without entering one of the well-tracked corridors.

Tonight, Paige wanted to talk with Kathleen.

"How did you do today?" Paige asked, sitting on the side of the bed.

"Pretty good, I guess. I'm slowing down just a tad and walking like I don't care where I'm going. In a week I'll blend in perfectly," Kathleen said, as she sat up in bed and lowered her legs over the side.

"Better make it two weeks," Paige said. "I've watched some people take three or four weeks before the drug takes full effect. I was watching you and you seem to be fitting in just fine. Just don't be too anxious to become a zombie because once you do, you can't go back to being normal," she warned.

"Okay, I'll slow it down."

"Did you see or hear any telephones?" Paige asked.

"No. I've been looking to see if there's a cell phone on any of the workers and I can't find one. I believe they have to leave them when they come to work. No one seems to have a phone with them at any time," Kathleen said.

"I'll bet half the people in here shouldn't be here," Paige said, waving her hands in exasperation. "And I'll bet some have been here for years. When they get really sick, they're shipped off to a hospital or a different home to die. Others may not even get the chance to go to the hospital. They just keep them here and let them die. If they can't walk or get around in a wheelchair, they're moved out. I believe this is a facility just to make money. There is no effort made to keep the patients healthy, to make them happy, to vary their diet or give them anything nice to eat. They don't even provide a TV or magazines to read. It's a house where crazy people are sent to live their last few years. The trouble is they don't live…they just exist. I haven't had a physical evaluation and I'll bet no one else has, either," Paige commented. "Have you?"

"Not that I'm aware of." There was a pause before Kathleen continued. "Paige, we're going to get out. I know my daughter-in-law will be looking for me."

"I thought she was the one who put you here," Paige said.

"I mean my first daughter-in-law…Carol. She's a gem and she'll know what Tillie has done. She'll figure it out. And when they come to take me, I'm going to insist they take you with us, also. I'll not go without you."

"Thank you, Kathleen," Paige said, squeezing her hand. "And if they rescue me first, I'll take you with me. In the meantime, just remember to remove that white pill every day. Now let's get some sleep."

CHAPTER TWENTY-EIGHT

"*M*rs. Larson, please take a seat," said James Belcher as Tillie followed him to his desk in a cubicle.

When both were seated, Belcher spoke. "Mrs. Larson, the authorization hasn't gone through yet for you to co-sign on your mother's checking account. This sometimes takes a few days. I made a mistake when I didn't ask you for a copy of the POA when you came here originally."

"It's been a few days. I thought I was being considerate waiting this long," Tillie huffed. She guessed this might have something to do with her brief conversation with the police, but decided to play it off and see what happened.

"Sometimes our administrators have to look at the authorization very carefully. My supervisor asked me to provide him with a copy of the power of attorney and I told him I hadn't requested that of you. I was told we need a copy before we can disperse any funds. Could you bring the original and a copy for us to review? If you bring it this afternoon, we can get to that right away," said Belcher.

"Well, I can't wait for them to take their good old time! Bills have to be paid," Tillie hissed, barely able to control her temper. There was a pause before she got up and scurried out of the bank without any further comment. She knew what this was all about and wondered if the police had already been notified.

Just as she reached the door, she turned to see Belcher on the phone with his head turned away.

Tillie knew what Belcher was doing, she didn't need to hear. Instead of taking a left turn out of the parking lot, she took a right and headed for the residential section of town, avoiding the main traffic arteries. In half an hour, she was at her own bank. Fifteen minutes later, she had several thousand dollars in cash and had closed her checking account. She stayed on side streets and made her way to the north side of town. Her black Mustang stood out in sharp contrast to the older cars and trucks parked at the Thrifty Inn.

Once inside, she paid the innkeeper cash and asked for a room as far from the street as possible. She had backed into the parking spot so her vanity tag that read, 'MINE' wouldn't be facing outward. She figured her tag was an easily identifiable sign; a black Mustang with the license plate 'MINE' would be easily remembered and reported.

She entered her motel room and breathed a sigh of relief. She needed time to make her plans and assess her situation and it would be much better if she wasn't disturbed.

I know they'll start shutting down access to my mother-in-law's assets, she thought. *In fact, they might start looking at my assets and try to prevent me from using those, too. I'll call my 401k account and have a check made out for all I've contributed. That should be quite a bit and I can save that check until I open up a new account someplace else. All I have to do now is get that check.*

It was slowly dawning on Tillie that she wasn't going to get all the money she had anticipated. In fact, her main concern was now to avoid jail. Deep down she believed as long as she knew where Kathleen was and they needed her to find her mother-in-law, she could make a deal. After all, the police would never find Kathleen without her help, would they? She hoped that would be enough to keep her out of prison.

After several inquiries as to whom she should contact, Tillie called the office that handled her 401k. When she finally got someone to speak with her, she was shocked by all the questions. Did she have any other 401k accounts, was she 59 and a half years old, and how quickly would she need the money? It was clear the employee was doing everything in her power to discourage Tillie from withdrawing the money. She even asked whether Tillie owned a home or had other assets she could count on temporarily for income.

"I just want you to write out a check and tell me where to pick it up," Tillie snapped. She was used to having her way and did not appreciate this delay.

"We usually send it to your place of business," explained the employee.

"I don't want you to do that. I'll come and pick it up."

"That is highly unusual, ma'am," the woman on the phone said hesitantly.

"I don't care what it is!" Tillie hissed in a near shout. "I'll come by your office this afternoon if you'll give me the address."

"Oh, I'm sorry. That's not how it works," the woman explained. "It will take some time to cut the check and then we will send it to your office or your residence by certified mail. Where do you want us to send the check? I'm looking at your office address now and would like you to confirm your residence if you wish us to send it there."

"Why can't I pick it up at your office?" Tillie asked.

"Because we are not equipped to have visitors. If you want us to send you your 401k funds, you'll have to follow our rules, just like everyone else," said the clerk.

Tillie slammed down the phone without uttering another word.

She left her motel room to clear her head and found herself walking on a busy street in a seedy part of town. It looked like a main road, but she didn't know or care which one. As she passed by an ABC store, she made up her mind to get some liquid refreshment. She left with Seagram's Seven, a blended whiskey she liked on previous occasions. That would be her only company this evening.

Two young men sitting at a bus stop saw Tillie come out of the ABC store with a brown bag in hand. When they got up from the bench, Tillie increased her pace and was thankful for the traffic that kept them on the other side of the street. Before they crossed the street, she turned into the motel parking lot and moved quickly to her room. Once inside, she closed the curtain, locked the door, and watched the street. She saw her pursuers stop on the street and finally retreat. It appeared she was safe for now.

CHAPTER TWENTY-NINE

*A*n All Points Bulletin had been put out on Tillie Larson immediately after she left the bank. The tip off for Belcher was Tillie's response when he required her to show him the original document. The report stated she was being sought in connection with unlawful detention and grand larceny. The detention charge got everyone's attention, because they assumed it was a child who was being detained.

The report also included a full description of Tillie's new black Mustang—and it was hard to miss a car like hers. Even the police would ogle sports cars whenever they saw them speed through an intersection. In fact, some officers were known to stop Mustangs just so they could talk to the owner about the attributes of their car. Officer Rogers wondered if Tillie was pleased with her purchase now that it was so easily identifiable.

Officer Rogers believed Tillie was still in town and had a judge give orders to put a hold on all her assets. Still sitting at the insurance office off Lakeshore Parkway, he dialed the number for Tillie's bank to make sure they'd received the hold notice. But it was too late.

"Son-of-a-bitch." Everyone in the office heard him even though the door was closed. Thinking he might have hurt himself, the receptionist stuck her head in the door.

"May I help you?"

"No. Sorry. I just overreacted." He didn't tell her he wasn't able to shut down one of Tillie's accounts in time and now she had several thousand dollars in cash. "Sorry."

Officer Rogers went back to his list of assets and made several more calls. When he called the office where Tillie Larson held her 401k, he received an earful from the young lady who had dealt with Tillie earlier.

"Did she leave a phone number?" Rogers asked.

"No, but it was a local call," the employee said, clearly exasperated. "She indicated she could be at my office in a short amount of time. The numbers I have for her are her office and residence. I don't have her cell phone. She slammed the phone down when I told her she couldn't come by to pick up the check and it might be several days before it was cut."

"And what time was it you last spoke with her?" Rogers asked.

This information helped Rogers confirm Tillie was still in town and had more business that needed her attention. He didn't say it, but appreciated the information Drew Stephens was able to provide since it helped him stay a step or two ahead of her. He was confident his associates would find her.

CHAPTER THIRTY

*T*illie didn't sleep well. The whiskey did put her to sleep just a few minutes after she turned off the TV, but around midnight, she was wide awake with all sorts of questions jumbling her thoughts. She picked up the half-empty whiskey bottle then reconsidered; her stomach and head told her she'd too much to drink already. She flipped channels looking for anything interesting and came up empty. She turned off the TV, then tossed and turned for another hour or so before sleep and the alcohol finally overtook her.

A gentle knock at the door awakened her.

"Yes," she responded instinctively. Daylight spilled in through a slit in the window curtain.

"Missy, you have gentlemen here to see you." It was the high-pitched voice of the owner.

"Tell them I'm not interested," she groaned.

A strong voice spoke next. "This is the police. Open up or we'll bust in the door."

The next ten seconds were enough for Tillie to decide she had no chance to flee. "Give me a few minutes to get dressed and I'll be right out."

The voice said, "Now you're being smart. We have the back covered and your car is being towed. I suggest you hurry."

When she opened the door, she was put in handcuffs, marched the ten feet to the lot, and seated in the back seat of a police car. An officer read her the Miranda rights and whisked her away to the Homewood jail with lights flashing and siren silent.

Down at the police station, Tillie refused to answer questions. She stated she wanted to speak with a lawyer, but didn't have one in mind. She would be required to wait until one was appointed for her. In the meantime, she was searched and given an orange prison uniform. A patrolman escorted her to a cell and told her she would remain there until a lawyer could be located. It was cool and she was concerned she might catch a cold. Finally, at five-thirty in the afternoon, a lawyer by the name of Anthony Robertson was seated in the visitor's room. It annoyed her that it took all day to get her representation.

A guard escorted Tillie to the small visitor's room where a desk and several chairs were provided. Lawyer and prisoner were seated on opposite sides of the desk.

Anthony was about thirty-five, five-foot eleven, and about two hundred pounds. Tillie guessed he was part Hispanic and black. His suit was crumpled and his tie slightly askew. He was quite handsome, or so Tillie thought, though a good suit would have improved his appearance greatly. He had a gentle way about him.

"Ms. Larson, I'm Anthony Robertson. What exactly are you being accused of?" he began.

"They are saying I falsified a durable power of attorney to steal my mother-in-law's assets."

"Did you?" After a very long pause, he added, "What you tell me is safe with me. I'm not your accuser. I'm here to give you the best legal advice."

Finally, she nodded after he asked the question again.

"Are there any other charges?" he asked.

"They are threatening to charge me with unlawful detention if I don't tell them where she is," Tillie huffed.

"And who is *she?*"

"My mother-in-law, Kathleen Larson."

"And why won't you tell them where she is?" Anthony asked.

"If I do that, I have no power to bargain. That's the only thing I know they want."

"Maybe so. But if you don't answer them, you may spend the rest of your life in prison. Suppose something were to happen to Ms. Larson today, while she's… wherever you put her. If she is harmed or dies, you will be in very serious trouble."

"I don't want to tell anyone where she is," Tillie whined, almost childishly.

"My advice is for you to come clean," Anthony said and then hesitated as Tillie stared a hole through him. "…Tell them where she is and answer all their questions. You are in no bargaining position and the situation will only worsen if you hold out on them."

"How much time do I have before I need to make a decision?" Tillie found it difficult to remain still while answering these questions. She was like the proverbial cat on a hot tin roof.

"They will most likely arraign you in the morning," said Anthony. "That is, they will charge you with a crime. Remember, unlawful detention is an extremely *serious* crime. Larceny is much less so. The judge may or may not allow you to go home on bail depending on how serious he believes the crime is. You are playing roulette with your life by remaining quiet. If they charge you with unlawful detention, the judge will not allow you bail and you may face jail time for a month or two or more. If they only charge you with falsifying a document, you may be able to post bond. It's your decision, but I believe the correct decision is to tell them what they want to know. That's my professional advice as your attorney of record."

"Let me think about my options." Tillie stood up to leave. "I'll decide by the morning what I need to do."

Anthony nodded. "I'll find out the time for the arraignment and represent you at that hearing if you decide to say nothing. We'll find out then what they are charging you with. Think about what I'm advising. This is a serious situation," he said as convincingly as he could. Then Anthony got up from his chair and called a guard who escorted Tillie back to the holding cell.

CHAPTER THIRTY-ONE

Sometime in the middle of the night, Kathleen awoke with a start. She didn't know where she was and it took a few moments until she was orientated. She soon realized a thunderstorm woke her. She lay there for almost an hour, entertained by the lightning show outside her window. She listened to Paige's gentle snore and wondered how she'd be rescued. Finally, when she could stand it no longer, she sat on the side of the bed, put on her slippers and royal blue bathrobe, and moved toward the door. She listened carefully for several minutes before moving into the hall, hugging the wall. She knew the camera wasn't aimed along the wall, so if she were careful, she could avoid detection.

Everything she did, she did slowly. If she was stopped she figured she'd act like she was sleep-walking. She didn't like the very slight shuffling sound caused by her slippers as she moved toward the common room.

When she reached the big room, it was deathly quiet. The lights were dim allowing Kathleen to see inside the well-lit administration offices. She knelt down behind one of the upholstered chairs and watched. All remained quiet. She concluded she was alone in the room and so moved closer to the mirrored wall, which was now as transparent as a window. She avoided the lights.

She made her way to the door used by the kitchen staff and servers. From this position, she could see most of the main administration room, yet remain in darkness lest anyone catch her. She saw a security guard sound asleep with his head in his hands in front of a bank of monitors. *He's being paid for this,* she thought with a sigh. He seemed to be the only one in the office. As she continued to look around for a landline, cell phone, or way out, what she saw instead, quite by accident, was the big key used to open the front door. It hung on a hook near the door that provided access to the control room, about fifteen feet from the security guard. The dark, oxidized color of the key was in sharp contrast to the sterile surroundings of the wall. It hung just an arm's length from the door.

How can I get that key? she thought. *If I had it now, I would open that front door, lock it behind me, and head for the road. It would probably be several hours before cars would be on the road, but I could hide until someone rescued me. I can do it, but not on a rainy night like this. I've got to do it, but how do I get into that office?*

While Kathleen contemplated her situation, someone came out of one of the offices. The woman was probably in her late thirties or early forties, wearing a white blouse and dark skirt that were in sharp contrast to her white face and black hair. Kathleen was immediately suspicious that her black hair came from a bottle. The woman's skirt was short, especially for someone her age. *She is definitely the person in charge,* Kathleen thought.

The woman must have said something to the security officer, because he was startled awake and appeared to protest that he wasn't asleep. His eyes were soon focused on the monitors as he continued to converse with his manager. Kathleen knew she would have to remain motionless for a while and ducked further behind the armchair. When she saw the guard get up, stretch, and walk toward the office where the woman was working, she took advantage of his distraction to head back toward her room.

Paige was still snoring. Kathleen hung up her bathrobe, took off her slippers, and tucked herself in. She was proud of the work she had done and what she had learned. She couldn't wait to share her new-found secrets with her roommate and now knew she would need to overcome quite a few difficulties if she wished to leave this prison disguised as a nursing home. For now, however, she closed her eyes and was asleep in minutes.

CHAPTER THIRTY-TWO

*T*he following morning, Tillie was escorted to the courtroom in an orange jumpsuit and seated with her attorney to wait for the judge. Anthony again asked her how she would plea and told her what he thought she should do. When the judge took the bench, Tillie listened to the charges leveled against her. The prosecuting attorney read from a paper that she was accused of, "falsifying a legal document for the purpose of stealing the assets of the defendant's mother-in-law, a Mrs. Kathleen Larson." Tillie grit her teeth, hoping there would be no other charges. She believed she could talk her way out of that charge since she didn't believe there were any witnesses and they would never find her mother-in-law to testify against her. It seemed to elude her that her reasoning was flawed. If they didn't find her mother-in-law, she would *really* be in trouble.

In the court of the Honorable Kathryn L. Harris, the prosecuting attorney continued with his presentation.

"We are also charging the defendant with unlawful detention." The prosecuting attorney continued with the rest of the charge while Tillie remained silent, staring straight ahead. She leaned over to her attorney who advised her to plead 'not guilty.' She nodded and very quietly uttered the plea.

"Would the defendant please speak up?" asked the judge.

"Not guilty," Tillie repeated, this time a bit too loud.

"Do you understand the charges, Mrs. Larson?"

She looked at her attorney who nodded his head and she said, "I do, Your Honor."

"It is my decision to deny bail until the location and condition of Mrs. Kathleen Larson can be ascertained. I also wish to see both attorneys in my chambers."

Tillie was returned to her cell and a short time later in the morning she was visited by Anthony Robertson. This time he came to her cell and spoke to his client through the bars. A guard stood at the end of the hall.

"I don't envy your position," he said as Tillie rolled her eyes. "This judge is not going to let you out on bail until Ms. Larson is returned to her family and her story is heard. If she isn't returned, you will spend the rest of your life in prison. Should something happen to Mrs. Larson that has nothing to do with you, or even if she does something that causes her own harm, injury, or death, you can be charged with being the principal cause of her injury or death." That might be cause for a long prison sentence.

"I need some time to think," Tillie grumbled.

"You'll have plenty of time to do that here. Just hope and pray she remains safe and no harm comes to her, because if it does, you may be looking at serious time. My advice is to tell everything, plead guilty, and admit this scheme got out of hand and you're sorry. You never intended to harm Mrs. Larson. Throw yourself on the mercy of the court. Anything else would be foolish. With the proper expression of sorrow and regret and the right amount of tears, you may possibly get off with ten years."

While Tillie didn't say it to Anthony Robertson, she was not inclined to take his advice. She figured the authorities would beg her to tell them where Mrs. Larson was, and would offer a more lenient sentence if she provided the necessary information. She honestly believed they needed her and that she was still in a good position to deal. She would, of course, make sure the deal was in writing before she told them what they wanted to know.

Anthony could tell Tillie was not buying a plea bargain. "You're playing with fire here, Tillie," he said. "And you're going to get burned. I've been around the criminal justice system for the last ten years. I've seen many miscarriages of justice. I've also seen many people who should have been convicted, get acquitted. But I have never seen anyone beat the system like you're trying to. They've got you and will soon have more than enough evidence to lock you away for good. Once again, my advice is for you to tell them where your mother-in-law is and what you did. Tell them you're sorry and you were foolish. Throw yourself on the court's mercy and hope they come down easy on you." With that last bit of wisdom, he turned his back on his client, asked the guard to open the door, and did not look back at the jail cell.

CHAPTER THIRTY-THREE

Sometime near mid-morning, Kathleen wandered around the common room. She made it appear as if she were not paying attention to where she was going, not that she had anywhere to go, for that matter. She did her best to meander like many of the other patients. She finally sat down in an upholstered chair, facing the door to the administration wing and the keypad that permitted its access. She lidded her eyes as if she were about to fall asleep.

The first person she observed entering the administration wing positioned herself in such a way that it was impossible to see her press the keypad. A second nurse also blocked the view with her body. Finally, after what felt like hours, a third person stood far enough away from the door to make it possible for Kathleen to clearly see the top key on the right being pressed. *The first number is three,* she thought. One more hour passed before another person used the keypad. She was able to confirm the first number was three and the second might have been the middle key, five. She waited another hour before she was able to get a good view of the pad being pressed. *It is five!*

Growing weary, Kathleen got up and wandered, as was expected of her, until lunch. She was careful to avoid sitting at the same table as Paige lest anybody suspect them. Lunch was the usual sliced bologna sandwich, some chips, and half an apple. She was learning to live with the predictable diet, even though she yearned for some good home-cooked food. About an hour after lunch, she took a seat in the same armchair near the administration door and once again gave the appearance she was taking a nap. She observed several people use the keypad, but still couldn't tell for certain what the last two numbers were. They were *eight, nine* or *nine, eight.* That would make the pass number either 3-5-8-9 or 3-5-9-8. In the next hour, she never got another good view.

As Kathleen rested in the big chair, she wondered what the weather was like. Since hardly anyone came through the big wooden doors, it was not possible to observe how people were dressed. She would have to rely on her memory and possibly the view from her bedroom window for some indication of the weather. February in Alabama could be cold or comfortable, depending on the vagaries of the jet stream. Often, it would be in the forties at night and reach the upper seventies during the heat of the afternoon. Kathleen didn't have a warm coat with her and suspected Paige didn't either. *When we get out of this place,* she thought, *we'll have to take our blankets with us, wear our sturdiest shoes, and put slacks on over our pajamas.*

The long afternoon led at last to dinner, a short quiet time after the meal, and finally to bedtime. Everyone was ushered to their rooms and staff members were available to see everyone was in the right room, since patients would sometimes get confused. After everyone was tucked in their own bed, the staff returned to their positions or prepared to go home.

Kathleen had concluded supper was early so patients could be put in bed early, allowing most of the staff to go home when that task was completed. In any case, when she looked out the window it was already dark and she saw no indication of precipitation. She had no idea if it was wet or dry, warm or cold, calm or windy. Not a single light shown outside her window on this moonless night.

It was becoming clear to Kathleen that what was done was done to save money. The staff was kept to a minimum and they worked long hours. There was a crew that worked the first four days of the week and a second crew that worked the weekends. The food was plain, inexpensive, and bland. What was worse, it was the same every day, with very little variation. There was no chef in the kitchen, only a pseudo cook who was willing to whip up plain food for seventy or eighty patients. Those who assisted the cook didn't mind doing dull, boring work.

Kathleen was surprised few people had colds or coughs. When she considered it, there was little reason why they should catch cold since the common room remained at a steady temperature, probably about 75 degrees Fahrenheit, and there was little contact with outsiders. She assumed it would be in the best interest of the nursing home to monitor the staff to make sure no germs were introduced that would harm the patients. The nursing home only got paid if those in their care remained alive and well. Besides, few of the staff came into close contact with the patients anyway.

After all had been quiet for about a half hour, Kathleen left her bed and sat on the edge of Paige's bed. Paige was still awake.

"Paige," she whispered. "I may be able to get the big key that opens the wooden door."

"How are you going to do that? How do you even know where the key is?" Paige asked, her voice heavy with suspicion.

"I've been busy the last few nights. I'm not positive I can get the key, but if I can, do you want to go with me, take our chances trying to get a car to pick us up?"

"I sure do. Count me in. I'll do anything to get out of this lousy place," Paige assured her.

"In an hour or so, I'm going to try to get the key. It might take a while since the security guard has to be asleep and there is a second person who is in those administration offices. I have to be patient," Kathleen said, wringing her hands.

"How are you going to get through that door? You have to know the code," Paige warned.

"I do, except for the last two numbers. I may have them mixed up. This afternoon I pretended to be asleep in one of those chairs near the mirror and was able to watch what keys were pressed. I have to wait until the guard is asleep and the night manager is in one of the offices."

"Oh, good!" Paige exclaimed, almost too loudly. "What can I do?"

"Be ready to leave with me. Dress as warmly as you can, piling on whatever you have, and we'll bring our blankets with us. Good shoes would be helpful. I hope we can do it tonight, if not we'll try again tomorrow."

"Good luck. I'll be ready. Just don't get caught."

"I'm going to wait for another hour or so. I want the security guard to be tired. That's when he took his nap last time. Get some sleep and I'll wake you when I get the key and we're ready to escape."

Kathleen got under the covers but didn't sleep. This was one of the most exciting things she had ever done and it was probably the most dangerous. She had the feeling she was overlooking something, but didn't know what. Just as she was about to drift off, a thought came to her. The big wooden door would make quite a bit of noise when she opened it. The security guard would hear it and put an end to their escape. This problem couldn't be ignored.

She sat on Paige's bed and gently shook her shoulder. "We can't go tonight," she whispered. "The door will make too much noise. We need to put some oil on the hinges or it will give us away. Let's think about this. One or two more days won't kill us. We've got to find a way to silence that door."

CHAPTER THIRTY-FOUR

*A*s Kathleen sat on the side of her bed, she saw the security guard's flashlight flicker down the hall. She fell back down on her bed and pulled the covers over her. For an instant, the flashlight searched her room before continuing on. Kathleen waited. Questions tormented her. She needed to know if the security guard checked every night or if this was an unusual procedure. She made a mental note of the moonlight's position on the floor and the fact it would be an hour later when it reached the same position tomorrow night.

She needed to tell Paige, but the morning would do. Kathleen's last thought before drifting back to sleep was she had to know the security man's schedule or she'd take a chance of running into him and ruining their plans. She would have all day tomorrow to figure it out.

The following evening came after what seemed a very slow day. Kathleen couldn't wait to find out if the security man would come around with his flashlight—

and if so, would it be at the same time? She sensed he was a creature of habit and that habit was to do only what was absolutely required.

When the moonlight reached the appropriate spot on the floor, she listened for the guard's footsteps and, sure enough, the glint of his flashlight sped across the two beds. *He* is *a creature of habit,* she thought. *So much better for us.*

The next night after the guard had made his rounds, Kathleen pulled back the covers and once again sat on the side of her bed, listening to the sounds of the night. This time, she decided to walk without slippers, even if the floor was cold on her feet. The slippers always made a slight shuffling sound, and now she felt more comfortable being able to move in complete silence. Plus, her sleepwalking excuse would sound more plausible if she were barefoot.

Kathleen stopped at the entrance to the common room. She didn't see the security guard snoozing in front of the monitors, but did see the night manager going about her business. The manager walked from the office to her file cabinets several times as Kathleen hid behind her usual chair. *Maybe the guard's off tonight,* she thought. *Nothing goes on, anyway. No I'll bet he's in one of those offices, taking his usual nap.* Hugging the wall, she moved toward the one-way mirror.

Something was wrong. She was halfway across the common room, almost to the one-way mirror, when the hairs on her arms stood up. She stopped, stood perfectly still, and looked all around her. Then all of a sudden, she heard noise on the couch not five feet from her. The security guard lay, a lump of dark blanket curled up in a heap on the couch. He had just turned on his side. She never thought to check the sofas and chairs, and now she was just several feet from being caught.

Afraid he might be semi-awake, she dared not move but pulled her bathrobe up over her face, making her almost invisible. Just then, the lady behind the glass moved toward the entrance and past the big key. Kathleen ducked down behind the couch, being careful to not touch it. The manager entered the hall.

She seemed to know where the security guard would be taking his nap, since she headed directly for the couch.

"Kenny," she whispered in a voice that scared Kathleen. It sounded to Kathleen like she was waking the dead. "Kenny...you've slept long enough. It's time for you to make the rounds."

"Oh, shit. I forgot. Okay, give me a minute," Kenny mumbled.

"Don't go back to sleep. Come on." The manager turned and headed back to her office.

"Don't worry. I'm awake." Kenny sat up on the couch, rubbed his eyes, and stood. He stretched and moved his waist in a circle before he headed for the administration area. Kathleen saw that he was about five feet ten inches, with a black beard and a military haircut. She estimated his age at about twenty-five.

Kathleen was still afraid to move. She didn't know where the guard was going first and wasn't sure if she should return to her bed. So, for now, she just knelt there behind the couch. A minute later, she heard the office door open and Kenny came out into the common room with a flashlight. He headed down the first corridor on the left that was labeled "A" high on the wall. A few moments later, he walked down corridor B.

Kathleen continued to kneel as Kenny came out of the second corridor and walked to the men's room. He turned on the light in the men's room and reentered the main room a minute later, remembering to turn off the light.

His next stop was the big front door. All he did was check the handle to make sure it was still locked. From there, he went into the ladies' room, turned on the light, and spent several minutes inside. His next destination was corridor C, which is where Kathleen and Paige were housed.

It didn't appear as if he spent too much time observing—it was more like a quick glance and a pause. He was just going through the motions. Still, Kathleen worried. *I wish I had stuffed something in the bed to make it look like I was sleeping,* she thought. *How could I miss this?* Her covers were still pulled back and Kenny would be able to tell in an instant that no one was in the bed. *I just hope he's as careless as I think he is.*

With the guard down the corridor, Kathleen found a better hiding place behind an arm chair approximately ten feet from the couch. Kenny came out of corridor C just a moment later. He must not have noticed anything out of order when he looked in Kathleen's room. *Yep. Kenny's a careless one, alright*, she thought.

When Kenny walked past the couch where he had been sleeping, he picked up the dark blanket and folded it over his arm. Then he completed his tour of corridor D before continuing on to the administration offices. Kathleen was pleased she had moved away from the couch since she forgotten about the blanket and he might walk into her quite by accident.

Finally, she could breathe. She waited another five minutes until she saw Kenny playing a game of FreeCell on the computer, and then it was time for Kathleen to head back to bed.

What she learned would help her and Paige in their escape. As she tiptoed back into her room, she leaned over Paige's bed and lightly tapped her shoulder until she was awake.

"Paige," she whispered.

"What?" grumbled Paige, still half asleep.

"I watched the guard! He makes his rounds of the corridors about midnight and he shines his flashlight in each room. We should make our beds look like someone is sleeping under the blankets. We'll have to time our escape after he makes the rounds, otherwise we might just bump into him as we try to leave. He comes down each corridor, so we'll wait until after he comes down ours. He's very quiet, but we'll see his flashlight."

"Great," said Paige, rolling over to face Kathleen.

"We're getting closer. Just a few more things to figure out," Kathleen said, wringing her hands.

"Tomorrow night or the next will be fine with me," said Paige. "Just as long as we get out of this terrible place. I can wait."

The next morning, Kathleen had her mind on other things when she bit into the white pill that was hidden amongst her grits. Her back was facing the administration wing and for that she was grateful as she took the pill out of her mouth and put it in her pocket. She suspected she may have swallowed a portion of the pill, but probably not enough to affect her.

An attendant in pink scrubs came by moments later. Kathleen had been careless and wondered if the nurse saw her put the pill in her pocket. Her heart beat fast and she prayed the attendant hadn't noticed anything unusual. The nurse in pink scrubs came to Kathleen's table and distributed her usual blood pressure pill, followed by a glass of water. She then moved her tray to the next table.

When her heartbeat returned to normal, Kathleen looked around for Paige but didn't see her. Then she saw something that once again quickened her pulse. Butter cups sat on the table as they always did for breakfast. But today they shone in a whole new light.

Kathleen took two of the plastic cups and quickly put them in her pocket. She left two on the table as most of the patients didn't use butter. As she got up from the table, she looked at a nearby table that was occupied by two ladies who were finishing the last of their toast. As she passed, she grabbed a third container. *Just in case,* she thought.

CHAPTER THIRTY-FIVE

Carol called Drew to find out what he knew about the search for Kathleen and what information Tillie had been able to provide. Since they both worked downtown, it was only natural they meet at one of the many restaurants on the south side of town. They chose Dreamland, famous for barbeque, and met at the restaurant about twenty minutes before noon to get a head start on the busy lunch crowd.

"What did you learn from Tillie?" Carol began the conversation while they were waiting for their sandwiches.

"As far as I can tell, nothing," Drew sighed, as he opened his paper napkin and placed it on the table.

"*Nothing?* Did she say anything at her arraignment?" Carol leaned forward in her seat.

"Yeah. Two words. 'Not Guilty.'"

"What about her attorney?" Carol asked, desperate for helpful information.

Drew shook his head. "Anthony Robertson is an ethical lawyer and wouldn't be inclined to betray his client. He wouldn't say anything that would harm her."

"So, we don't know anything?" Carol asked, nodding at the waitress who refilled her water glass.

"I did hear from one of the guards that she's not talking," Drew offered. "It seems her attorney is frustrated because she won't listen to his advice. The guard said the attorney leaves meetings with her, muttering to himself. That's all I've been able to learn."

Carol wrung her hands. "Damn it. I wonder how my mother-in-law is doing. Is she eating well and being treated right? Is she still in Alabama or did something terrible happen to her? I worry about her."

"I know this is hard on you. I've had my secretary call all the nursing homes that are restrictive in a four-county area and inquire about a Kathleen Larson. We both suspect she's being held under another name since our inquiry turned up nothing," said Drew.

Carol slammed her hands down on the table. "That's it! I'll bet Tillie and whoever she's working with gave Kay a new name and listed her under an alias. Especially now they know we're looking for her."

Drew nodded. "Whoever is harboring her knows what he or she is doing. This is probably not the first time they've held someone against their will and without cause. I don't think it'll make a difference if they know someone's looking for her. They probably expected that, otherwise they wouldn't have changed her name. I'll bet the reason Tillie wanted the power of attorney was to make it seem legal to put Kathleen away. The nursing home couldn't take her unless they had a POA certificate."

"You're right. I think that's why she was pushing so hard for that authority," Carol said, staring straight ahead. "She would also need the power of attorney to get access to all of Kay's assets, especially the Vanguard account. Do you think Kay's in any danger?"

"I don't think so. She's probably being fed and has a place to sleep. I think Tillie is a crook, but not a murderer. She must know that if a person dies while in custody, the punishment is much more severe. But who knows if she's getting her medication at a place like that. Some of the seedier nursing homes even use drugs to get the patients to sleep and remain docile," he said.

"That's what scares me," said Carol. "Kathleen was such a happy person, full of piss and vinegar. It makes me sick to think she's shut away someplace with no one to talk to, no friends, and no mental stimulation." They paused as the waitress brought their sandwiches and soft drinks to the table.

"It's my hunch we will eventually find her and she'll be no worse for wear," said Drew. "She's a tough lady and she'll survive this. We're not going to give up until we find her. Tillie thinks she has the upper hand because she knows where Kathleen is. What she doesn't know is we won't quit until we find her. We have the upper hand. Now let's eat and get back to work," Drew said as if he were annoyed.

"One last question...What do you think is Tillie's real motive? Is she trying to kill Kay?"

"No," said Drew, taking a sip of his drink. "She's after Kathleen's money. Tillie doesn't really care about her but is jealous of what she has...especially now that she was awarded the seventy thousand. She wants her money. But she *will* kill her if she doesn't talk. Kathleen can't live in a place like that without going crazy. Don't worry, Carol, we'll find her."

CHAPTER THIRTY-SIX

*T*he following evening, armed with the knowledge of Kenny's schedule, Kathleen waited until she saw his flashlight shine down their corridor. After he finished his rounds, she left the bed and put her pillow under the covers to make it look like someone was in the bed.

"Paige," she whispered. "I'm going now. This may take a while, so don't get anxious. You may want to wait for me to return before we dress for our trip outside. Wish me luck."

Paige gave her a 'thumbs up' as Kathleen slipped out the door.

Hugging the wall and barefoot as before, she stopped at the entrance to the common room. She waited for her eyes to dilate before checking the arm chairs to make certain no one was taking a snooze in one. Then she moved along the perimeter toward the mirrored wall, staying in the shadows and only moving when Kenny was not focused on the monitors. She could see the night manager moving between the file cabinets and copy machine in the main room and one of the three offices. Tonight, Kathleen wore a dark blue nightgown, making her less visible than previously. For extra security, she wrapped her bathrobe around her throat and mouth.

It occurred to Kathleen that Kenny wouldn't nap while the manager was busy in the main room. Only when she retired to one of the offices and concerned herself with her work did he cradle his head. Eventually she didn't see the woman and noticed the guard had begun to nod off. It was as if he and his manager had a mutual understanding: he wouldn't nap when she was in the big office and she wouldn't bother him during a certain hour of the night. That time was shortly after his rounds.

Kenny's computer sat next to the monitors and Kathleen watched his eyelids grow heavier and heavier as he contemplated his next move in FreeCell. She found that five minutes seemed like five hours when you were anticipating doing something so daring. After what felt like an eternity, the guard got up from his chair, looked in the office, and sat once more. He put his head down on his arm and, in another five minutes, his breathing was heavy as if in deep sleep.

Kathleen crept closer to the door and removed the now melted butter cups from the pocket of her robe. She had to step on her toes to reach the highest hinge. She poured about half the cup on the lower part of the hinge, but most oozed down the door. Tall Paige would have to finish the job. Frustrated, she quickly buttered the other hinges and slipped the cups back into her robe.

Her next chore and the most difficult was to steal the key. Kathleen moved quietly toward the administration offices where she could see the key hanging on the wall inside the door. She picked up two small pillows from a nearby chair and set them to her side. Moving noiselessly to the keypad, she pressed 3-5-9-8 and got a message that said 'Incorrect.' *Damn,* she thought. *Focus.* She tried a second time, reversing the last two numbers, and the door opened. She held it open for a moment, listening to see if there was any movement inside the offices. She was rewarded with silence.

Kathleen didn't know if she needed to know another code to get back through the door, and was afraid the door might make too much noise if she pressed the bar that usually opened it. She didn't want to take any chances, so when she went through the door, she wedged it open with a couch pillow. She opened the next door very carefully, peeking through to observe a still-sleeping guard. She could hear the clicking of computer keys in the background and smell the stale aroma of coffee. The night manager was working away in her office next door. With one hand on the door, Kathleen opened it enough to squeeze through. She thought she could hold the door open and reach the key, but her arms couldn't reach both. She would have to enter the room. She backtracked, retrieved the second couch pillow, and placed it in the door opening. One long step and her hand touched the big key hanging on the wall. Its heavy iron clunked against the wall and she froze.

The heavy iron key was cold to the touch and she froze when she heard Kenny yawn. That was followed by a shuffle and Kathleen knew she would have to retreat. She didn't have the key, but had to close the door or she would be exposed. She passed through the door, taking the pillow with her and put her hand on the latch. Then, with the utmost care, she closed the door the rest of the way, with her hand still pressing down on the latch. She heard movement inside and released the latch, barely making a sound.

Tonight would not be the night.

Safe in her room, Kathleen tiptoed to the foot of her roommate's bed and whispered, "Paige, I wasn't successful. Both the guard and the lady in charge didn't cooperate. I had my hand on the key, but almost got caught. I had to leave the key so they wouldn't see me."

In a soft voice Paige replied, "I'm so glad you didn't get caught. Let's plan on tomorrow night."

"That's a good idea. I've had enough excitement for one night. I found out tonight that we *can* escape from this nut house," Kathleen said, letting out a laugh.

"Then one day won't make a difference. I'm glad you're being cautious. I worry about us getting caught," said Paige.

"I'm being careful. Tomorrow we'll leave this place. Knowing we can do it is truly exciting."

Kathleen walked over to the barred window between the beds and observed a clear night with a moon that was about half way through its cycle. She hoped the next night would be as clear and they'd have the moon to light their footsteps.

"I'll bet we'll be successful tomorrow night," Kathleen said. "Now I'm ready for sleep."

Both women, in darkness, experienced a sense of elation, knowing tomorrow evening might be the night of their deliverance.

Kathleen was not in bed but five minutes when a thought made her bolt upright. *The butter!* For a moment she nearly panicked, but then laughed aloud as she realized a little butter on the door would not, in fact, be out of place.

CHAPTER THIRTY-SEVEN

The head nurse at Lakeside Nursing Home, Inez Lee, car pooled with the assistant nurse, Maggie Pope. Inez drove an old Ford sedan that provided her dependable transportation. It was black, not very pretty, but trustworthy. She treated the car well, only drove it for work and shopping. She had a mechanic boyfriend who made sure it was serviced properly.

As they were coming down I-65 south to the nursing home, the two ladies weren't doing much talking. That was unusual since both were normally loquacious, chattering away about the previous evening.

This morning Inez was unusually quiet and Maggie wondered why. "What'cha thinking, Inez? Somethin's bothering you," she said. Both women were in their mid twenties. Maggie was a bit over weight, but she didn't let it bother her. In fact, she thought it was sexy. She had a nice smile and genuinely liked people.

Inez was the thinker. She went to college and became a licensed practical nurse...an 'LPN.' She kept her weight down and was happy with her job, her life, and her boyfriend.

"Yeah. Something is," said Inez, drumming her fingers on the wheel. "Yesterday I spoke to that new lady, Helen Parsons. I called her name four or five times and she never answered. It was like her name wasn't Helen. She heard me, but I could swear 'Helen' wasn't her name. She made me feel funny," said Inez.

"You know how the patients are." Maggie reached over and turned the radio down. "After they've been with us a few weeks, that little white pill starts to do its magic and they become very passive."

"Nah. It was like she was saying, even though she didn't speak, 'You're crazy. My name ain't Helen. You should know that.' She made me feel like I was the crazy one," said Inez.

"That's unusual. Normally I don't get any response when I talk with patients. Most of them just seem to understand and do what we ask them to do."

"You know what I'm thinking, Maggie?" asked Inez. "I'm thinking her name ain't Helen. I think that is the name they gave her so they could keep her in this place. When she first arrived, there was nothing wrong with her I could see. She even asked Georgia if she could find her something to read, a book or magazine. When Georgia gave her a book, they even had a conversation. Georgia said she was polite and seemed alert. Now Miss 'Helen' doesn't respond to her name and acts like all the others. That white pill sure does a job on them. Turns them into zombies," Inez said, shaking her head.

"Maybe they called her 'Helen' so when anyone inquires about her, Dr. King can say, 'We have no one by that name.' I wouldn't put it past Dr. King to keep someone here who shouldn't be in this place," Maggie offered.

Inez nodded. "That's what I'm beginning to think. Let's just watch and maybe we'll find out more. It's nice to know someone feels the same way about the place and how our patients are treated. There's so much more that could be done to make them comfortable and happy. I've never worked in a place that provided so little for patients."

The two continued to discuss their work at the nursing facility, right until they arrived at the home. Inez drove around to the back and maneuvered into her usual parking spot. Maggie pressed the buttons on the keypad and held the door open for Inez. Once inside, they put their cell phones in a wicker basket, not to be taken into the common room.

CHAPTER THIRTY-EIGHT

Kathleen and Paige once again ate breakfast at different tables. They didn't want the staff to link them together. Yet both wondered at various times during the day how nice it would be to have someone to talk with throughout the endless hours. The time would pass so much faster.

As breakfast was ending, a lady in pink gave Kathleen her blood pressure pill, as usual. As far as the staff was concerned, the only other medication she needed was the dreaded white pill. Now she was planning to leave this miserable place, she was observing things she hadn't observed before. She was surprised no one ever took her blood pressure or asked her what other medication she took.

When Kathleen lived at home, she would take a pill in the morning to keep the inflammation from arthritis from slowing her down. It was not a prescription, but rather an over the counter medicine. She didn't really have to take it, though it did make her life a little less painful while she was doing her job. Here, she didn't seem to need it as she did precious little each day except walk around the common room and nap. But she wondered how long her blood pressure would stay normal since it was not being monitored. She also wondered if anyone cared.

Kathleen made certain to stay away from the mirrored wall. She didn't want the staff to think she had any interest in that part of the room. Instead, she walked and napped and blended in with the other patients. Since she'd missed several hours of sleep the previous night, she actually did fall asleep several times during the morning.

While awake, Kathleen would sit, stare, or get up and walk to a new location. Life inside Lakeside Nursing Home was life devoid of stimulation of any kind. It was a recipe for dying. Kathleen thought, *This is a legal way of euthanizing people. Immoral, cruel, but legal. While dementia is not a state anyone would want to experience, taking away all visual and auditory stimulation will surely encourage an early death.*

At lunchtime, Kathleen noticed a lady several tables from her had fallen over on her side, with her face resting on the table. She didn't know if the lady was sick, dead, or had just fallen asleep. She wanted to go over and assist in any way she could, but knew she couldn't do that without revealing she was unmedicated. Five minutes passed and still no one noticed or came to assist the fallen lady. A man next to her got up and moved to another table. Finally, a nurse in a white uniform came over to ascertain the problem.

The nurse put her fingers on the patient's neck and shook her head. Then she went into the back room and came back with a stretcher and two attendants in pink. Ever so unceremoniously, the lady was lifted onto the stretcher and taken through the steel door to the administration and medical wing.

What a terrible way to die, Kathleen thought. *Alone, with no one to talk to, not even able to say she's suffering or feeling discomfort or wanting to lie down. Not having anyone who gives a damn, might be the worst part. Who was this lady? Was she a mother, a wife, a grandmother? Who were her friends and who will grieve for her passing? Will she be honored with a service and a eulogy? Or will she simply be disposed of at the convenience of those obligated to 'love' her?* Kathleen said a prayer for the lady before finishing her bologna sandwich.

CHAPTER THIRTY-NINE

*A*nthony Robertson hadn't called on Tillie Larson in three days and was showed to the visitor's room ahead of his client. He hoped a few days in confinement would lessen her resolve to stonewall those who were trying to resolve the situation. The prosecuting attorney had her all but tied up and buried, while the judge was determined she would remain in jail until her mother-in-law was found and safely returned to her family. And that family didn't include Tillie.

Tillie entered the room dressed in the usual orange jumpsuit. Anthony figured that humiliation would encourage Tillie to be a bit more flexible. But he couldn't remember when he'd had a more recalcitrant client. Most of the clients he represented were frightened teens or young men in their early twenties who believed they were tough. They presented a hard-hitting façade but many were soft underneath. Those who were new to the criminal justice system didn't know what to expect and often appeared to not care or behaved as if they were totally innocent and society was picking on them. They were undisciplined and only looking out for number one. This was not the case with his present client. Tillie actually thought she was doing what was in her own best interest.

Tillie Larson was cold and calculating and believed she was smarter than everyone. She had convinced herself she would come out of this with only a little bit of difficulty because she held all the cards. The way she saw it, she might just be given a gentle slap on the wrist.

"Good morning, Tillie," Anthony greeted her as she came in.

"Morning," she said, only because she had to.

"Have you given any thought to your situation?"

"Given any thought? It's all I think about. If they want to see that lady again, bring me a deal," she said, practically spitting the words out.

"Tillie, 'that lady' is your mother-in-law and it was you who did her wrong. The only way you can make this right is to cooperate. Remember, I'm not prosecuting you. I'm trying to help you." Anthony spoke softly but was furious inside.

"You're wrong. If they think they are going to find her without my help, they're mistaken. They need me or else *that lady* will die. Bring me a deal that keeps me out of jail and I'll tell them where she is."

Anthony took a deep breath before responding.

"You're delusional, Tillie. They would never do that. As your lawyer, I'll try to get you the very best deal. But you need to cooperate. Tell them where she is, restore all you have stolen, and hope she isn't hurt or dead. If she is, you may be looking at ten years to life."

Tillie shook her head. "Talk to the prosecution again and tell them I'm ready to deal if they ever want to see Kathleen Larson. That may be my only card, but without my help they will be instrumental in letting an innocent person die. Tell them to make me a deal," she almost shouted.

Anthony left the jail and walked to meet with the prosecuting attorney who had an office in city hall. The gentleman was available and welcomed Anthony into his office.

The space was generous and provided a view of both downtown Homewood and the new condominiums recently built behind the jail. The room was full of light and two potted plants sat near the window—a colorful croton and a fichus. The attorney sat behind a beautiful mahogany desk with a glass top over it. A carved wooden nameplate told us that he was Winston Grump.

"Well, Anthony, have you been able to talk any sense into your client?" he asked.

"I just came from the jail. She wants a deal. She'll tell us where Mrs. Larson is living in return for no jail time. I told her I would present the deal to you," Anthony said with a heavy sigh.

Winston chuckled, "You know I would never accept that deal. If she thinks she will not spend at least five years in prison, she may be crazy. I'm thinking ten and if the woman is in any way harmed or comes to an untimely death, we'll be recommending life in prison.

How can she imagine she'll not do prison time?" asked the prosecuting attorney.

"She thinks you'll cave because if you don't, Mrs. Larson will die. Somehow, Tillie believes she has the stronger position. I suspect Kathleen is well hidden if Tillie thinks she can take a chance like that. All I can tell you is she wants a deal and without it, she won't have anything to say." Anthony folded his hands together and waited.

"Here's the deal," the attorney leaned forward toward Anthony. "A minimum of five years plus five years' probation. And that's if we find the woman in good health, everything is restored, and Tillie behaves herself in prison. That's the best I can do and I've never made a sweeter deal for such a serious crime. Tell her that's my best offer and the only reason I'd consider it is because I'm concerned for Mrs. Larson."

"I can tell you what she'll say, but I'll tell her," Anthony said. "In the meantime, the police better double their efforts to find where Tillie has Kathleen stashed. I've even started thinking she might be out of state. Tillie is not giving me any hints. I wonder if that notary public might have some information?"

"I'll get one of the detectives on it right away. Tell Tillie, that's my best offer."

With that, Anthony shook hands with Winston Grump and left to bring the proposal to Tillie.

CHAPTER FORTY

*T*oday, the time between lunch and supper felt like the longest four hours of Kathleen's life. She watched Paige out of the corner of her eye while she pretended to sleep. Paige was truly an actress. She blended in like she had lived there for years. She didn't appear to notice anything, ignored the staff as if they were just other patients, walked like she was half asleep, and when she got tired, found a chair and stared at nothing. Kathleen realized Paige must keep her sanity by acting. She stayed in character for the entire duration of each day's play, made up of Act I, II, and III—more frequently called Morning, Noon, and Night.

When the lights came on in the common room, Kathleen recognized the signal for supper. She didn't look forward to the meal, but rather what might lie ahead. Would this night finally be their last in this awful prison?

She had spent the day thinking about what would happen after they left the home. *It's not a long walk to the main road*, she thought. *We could walk that in about ten minutes or less.* The roads would likely be empty at that hour, however, and any driver who happened to come by would probably be reluctant to stop for two crazy old ladies in blankets.

Kathleen remembered coming to Lakeside from the south and knew that was the way she should return. She couldn't remember how many miles they were from the highway, though, and wondered if they would need food and water, or a flashlight.

Kathleen was the first one at the table for supper. As other servings were placed on the table, she took a roll from a plate and placed it in her dress pocket, using her body to prevent anyone behind the mirror from observing. When the server placed the next patient's plate on the table, she stole their roll, as well. The patients at her table were not aware part of their meal had been stolen. There would be no easy way to store the milk, so Kathleen would just have to remind Paige to hydrate before they left the home and to dress with as much clothing as she could put on.

When evening recreation time was over, a bell rang and everyone moved toward their rooms. Patients in wheelchairs were delivered to their beds, along with those who were confused or couldn't remember where they were supposed to go. What was recreation for Kathleen and Paige was the end of their need to act. They were at last free to be themselves, even if their venue was not their choice.

Ten minutes later, the common room was totally empty, except for a staff member or two, and the lights were turned down. Chairs were rearranged and tables washed. It was now possible to see behind the mirrored glass and would be more so when the lights were turned off for the night. Staff went about the task of getting the patients into bed. The little white pills they took each morning would keep them asleep all night.

Soon, the staff members were on their way to their vehicles for a quick drive and an evening at home. A skeleton crew stayed behind for another hour or so.

It was just six o'clock, however, because it was February, it would be dark outside.

Kathleen and Paige dressed for bed, knowing a staff member would make sure they were ready for sleep. Sure enough, a nurse came to their room, heard the toilet flush, and saw they were in their pajamas and ready for sleep.

"Goodnight, ladies," she said, leaving the door partially open.

A moment later, a hand reached inside the door and turned off the light. Kathleen noticed it was dark outside and wondered if there would be a moon. It would be nice to have some light to help them stay on the road.

CHAPTER FORTY-ONE

*A*bout a half-hour after Kenny made his usual midnight rounds, Kathleen approached Paige's bed. "Paige, I'm going to try again to get the key."

"How long do you think it will take?" asked a sleepy Paige.

"That's difficult to say. It all depends if Kenny takes a nap and if he's left alone to sleep."

"Don't worry about me. I'll be dressed to travel. Take as much time as you need and for goodness sake, don't get caught," said Paige.

"Now would be a good time to dress," Kathleen suggested. "I suspect it will be cold outside, so wear what you can. I'll dress when I get back with the key."

Kathleen pushed open the door to their room and returned it to the same position after she was outside. She moved slowly, staying close to the wall and away from any light. She was barefoot as usual and stopped at the entrance to the common room to silently observe the shadows. She was relieved when she saw Kenny looking at the bank of monitors. After a thorough check of the room, she moved inside and to her left. She was not as frightened as she had been the evening before, having practiced once and knowing what she could expect. Yet she also knew her success would depend on luck. Kenny would have to take a nap if she were to reach the key.

Near the mirror, she could see Kenny and the night manager talking in the main office. Both had coffee cups in their hands and seemed like they were in no rush to get back to work. Kathleen took a seat in a chair that was in the darkest part of the room and considered going to sleep, but was afraid to take that chance. She knew Kenny was no stranger to snoozing on the couch.

In a moment, Kenny went to play games on his computer and Kathleen knew it wouldn't be long before he'd take his nap. It was another fifteen minutes before he put his arms down on the desk and placed his head on his arms, and it was another five minutes before she could see him breathing deeply. It was time to move.

Kathleen crawled beneath the mirrored window to the steel door, picked up two pillows along the way, typed in the numbers 3-5-8-9, and was rewarded with a soft click. She pushed the door open and placed a pillow where it allowed the door to close most of the way. Then she moved to the office door and very gently opened it and entered. Had Kenny been awake, he could have seen her. She placed the other pillow between the door and jam, gently closing the door. A water bottle sat in the wastebasket next to the door and she picked it up and placed it in her dress pocket before reaching for the key. She quietly removed the key from the hook on the wall, and was absolutely silent in her actions as she knew this was the most critical part of her evening. She again opened the door, crawled out backwards, removed the pillow and slowly allowed the door to close, holding down the door handle and letting it up, ever so gently. She now crawled toward the common room, pulled the door open and removed that pillow as she continued to crawl into the big room, letting the door close with a click. She watched Kenny to see if he heard the noise, and fortunately, he wasn't disturbed.

Kathleen could hardly believe it. She returned the pillows to the couch, she had accomplished all she'd set out to do. The guard still slept with his head resting on his arms and she couldn't see the night manager. She had almost reached her corridor when she heard voices. She stopped to take one last look. Kenny and the manager were now talking. Kathleen stood still for fear her motion would show up on one of the monitors. It seemed like eternity that she waited; she was so anxious to get back to her room and let Paige know she had been successful. Finally, she saw Kenny get up and walk around the room while talking with his supervisor. She moved quickly down the corridor and finally reached her room.

Paige was waiting for her. "Kathleen, I'm dressed like a mummy. I put everything on I could. How did you do?" she whispered.

"Ta, daaa! I've got the key," she whispered. She held it up so Paige could see and the two women high-fived. There was some light in the room as the moon was providing light to the grounds outside. "I also found a water bottle. It's only a sixteen-ounce bottle, but that should do us for a while. Plus, I have rolls under my pillow. I stole those at supper time."

"You are such a good thief. I'm proud of you," Paige said. "Are we ready to leave?"

"As soon as I get dressed we'll be ready. Let's drink some water so we don't have to drink what we'll take with us."

"Good thinking. I'll take a drink, too," said Paige.

Cloaked in three dresses, a sweater, shoes, and two pair of socks plus her jacket, Kathleen indicated she was ready to travel. They also took the dark blue blankets off their beds and draped them over their shoulders. Then they stuffed pillows under the sheets to make it look like people were in the beds. She took one last swig of water and filled the plastic container up to the top. Kathleen led the way and hugged the wall, moving quietly and slowly down the corridor. Kathleen had traveled this hall many times and was aware that cameras didn't reach sleeping quarters, only the common room. They moved slowly as they didn't want to wake any of the patients; their shoes made more noise than bare feet or slippers.

Once at the common room, they stopped and both could see the guard more or less paying attention to the monitors. By a gesture, Kathleen let Paige know they would have to wait. This was the first time Paige had seen inside the administration office, and she admired Kathleen's smarts for planning this breakout. When Kenny looked away from the monitors to speak to his manager once more, the two patients headed for the big wooden door.

The area around the door was shrouded in darkness. This was perfect for their escape, but forced Kathleen to find the opening for the key with her hands. She was anxious to see how buttering the hinges had helped. She turned the key ever so slowly, making as little noise as possible, then, looking back at the mirrored wall one last time, she pulled the door slowly toward them. She was certain the butter helped decrease the noise.

First it was two inches, then six inches, then a foot and a little more until they could squeeze out the door. Paige went first, then Kathleen. Paige closed the door and Kathleen locked it behind them. She had extracted as much pleasure as she could from this breakout and wanted to confuse the administration as much as possible. She hoped their message would speak loud and clear, "We weren't crazy!"

"I don't remember being so proud of any other achievement in my lifetime," Paige whispered. "This will be something we can write in our Christmas letter to family and friends next year. No one will have a story as good as ours. Kathleen, you're the greatest."

Kathleen chuckled. "I'm with you. Regardless of how this works out, we did a very special thing. We escaped from a mental home, something we couldn't do if we were mentally ill. Now, let's not get caught. I sure as hell don't want to go back," she said, as they began their walk.

"Me neither. They would really make it tough on us if we were caught. You showed me a very special side of you, Kathleen. You're smart and have guts. Few people could have done what you did. I'm proud to be your friend," Paige said, patting her on the back.

It was just past two in the morning as the two ladies, looking like homeless crazy people, made their way down the driveway, certain they would end up in a better place.

CHAPTER FORTY-TWO

The moon was late in its cycle, a crescent. It was still overhead, but leaning toward the western skyline, and tonight, it was playing 'peek-a-boo' with the clouds. As their eyes adjusted to the darkness, the light from the moon made it easy for Kathleen and Paige to see the circular driveway that led to the county road. It must have been two o'clock, give or take a half hour, when they reached the end of the driveway. Living in a place where time means nothing can disorientate a person. Time had become meaningless.

"Kathleen, I'm amazed," Paige whispered. "You got us out of there all by yourself and your brains. I can't believe it. Even if we get caught or die from the cold, I'll be forever grateful." The two women with blankets over their shoulders looked like refugees as they moved quickly down the macadam road toward the main road.

"We're not going to get caught or die from the cold," Kathleen laughed. "Just think…we're free! We'll make it. By the way, we can talk normal. We don't have to whisper."

"And we can walk normal instead of imitating crazy people," Paige said, also letting out a chuckle.

The two women skipped and patted each other on the back to signal their pleasure at being free. Paige took Kathleen's hand and the two were able to walk as they did before they entered the nursing home. It felt wonderful after so many days of having to shuffle, making believe they were zombies. It was especially pleasant for Paige as she had spent several months acting the part.

"It's nice to be able to talk without anyone hearing us," said Kathleen, stretching her arms. "I'm not certain which way we should go, but I came from the south and I think it might be best to return that way."

"I was drugged when I came here, so I have no idea which way is best. It's your decision," Paige said.

"We'll go south," Kathleen decided as they turned onto the main road. "I'd like to put as much space between us and this place as we can. The folks at the home will think we're two old demented ladies who won't be able to travel very far or fast. But maybe we'll meet someone or a car will pick us up. As it gets near morning, we'll have to be careful. Lakeside staff members will be coming to work and might recognize us," Kathleen warned.

"Even though we look like Indians on the Trail of Tears?" Paige laughed.

"Right," Kathleen smiled. "Really, though, we'll have to stay off the roads when it gets light. On second thought, I don't think anyone will stop to pick us up looking like we just came from the crazy house."

"You're right—we do look crazy! When the Lakeside people find out we're gone, they'll probably notify the authorities and tell them we're dangerous or something."

"We probably look like inmates from an asylum... which of course, we are," Kathleen said as she trudged along.

"Bye the way, are you warm?" asked Paige.

"So far, I'm comfortable. As long as we keep walking, we'll won't get too cold. How about you?"

"I'm fine," Paige said. "I'm glad it's not any colder and there's no wind. We'll be okay."

"If we can get a cell phone, I'll call my daughter-in-law. She can help us," said Kathleen.

"Isn't she the one who put you in Lakeside?" asked a confused Paige.

"No, this is the good daughter-in-law. The other one is evil. Carol knows how to do things and she would help us. *Tillie* is the one who had me committed. Now...how do we get a cell phone?"

"We don't have any money. Someone is going to have to help us, maybe at a convenience store." Paige concluded.

The two women kept talking as they walked at a fairly brisk pace of about three miles per hour. Paige was able to estimate how fast they were moving since she used to walk with a fitness group at the rate of one mile every twenty minutes. They were soon able to put quite a few miles between themselves and the home, though they hadn't seen a car all night. There was no doubt about it, they were out in the country.

Sometime near five o'clock, Paige suggested they take a break. The moon was moving toward the western horizon and providing only sporadic light. "I see some pine trees over there and a place where we can hide if we need to," she said. "We can put a blanket on the ground and put the other one over us and we'll stay warm."

At that moment, they heard a motor in the distance. They moved to the side of the road, and when they saw the lights on the bend up ahead, they ambled toward a hill and stood behind a pine tree with their blankets draped over their heads. The pickup truck passed. It was driving on the wrong side of the road and they were relieved they'd let it pass by.

"I could use a rest and I'm thirsty. How would you like a roll for breakfast?" suggested Kathleen.

"I have no idea how you stole two rolls. Didn't anyone see you?" Paige asked.

"I chose a table where no one else had taken a seat as yet. I just took two rolls and put them in my dress pocket. When a patient sat down, they didn't notice a roll was missing. It's that white pill, you know."

"Goodness, I'm tired," said Paige, slowing her steps.

"I'm tired, too, Paige," Kathleen said, handing her a roll. "I think we're safe for a while. No one will believe we walked this far. In fact, they have no idea when we left, what direction we went, or if we're even still on the grounds. Let's find a spot that's a bit deeper in the woods so we won't be seen."

"Fine. I'm really sleepy." Paige said, as she started up the hill.

"You know, it's not really that cold. I'll bet the temperature is in the forties or maybe even fifty," Kathleen said as she looked around for a place to rest.

"Paige," Kathleen continued, "You said you think the people at Lakeside will call the authorities in the morning. I don't think they will. They wouldn't want the police to inquire into the escape of two crazy people. There would be too many questions they couldn't answer. No...they'll come looking for us themselves. We're going to be okay."

"Now you've explained it, I think you're right," Paige said, her breath growing heavy as they climbed up the hill. "If they weren't doing anything wrong, they would call the authorities. Since they are engaged in illegal stuff, they'll come looking for us themselves."

"That's my feeling, too. Let's find a spot to rest."

They continued to climb until they reached a crest where they could see the road and extensive woods. The moonlight created shadows as it passed through branches, and they had to walk carefully so as not to step in a hole. Finally, they found a spot that was perfect: a pine forest of about fifty trees that provided a soft blanket of pine straw upon which to rest. Next to them was a clearing of wild azaleas that had just begun an early bloom. It felt more secure being off the road.

In the moonlight, Kathleen was able to find two sticks shaped like a 'Y.' She stuck those two sticks in the ground and placed a straight stick over them. Then, arranging a blanket over top, she created a shelter of sorts. Half a blanket covered the pine straw and the other half covered the travelers as they slept spooned together for the next several hours.

CHAPTER FORTY-THREE

*A*lexander King sat at his desk, having just finished his second cup of coffee since coming to work. He was presently about to finish reading the business section of yesterday's newspaper when there was a strong knock at his door.

"What?" he said with a huff, refusing to take his eyes from the paper.

A young lady, the supervisor from the kitchen group, opened the door. She hesitated, trying to find a good way to begin. She wasn't sure how to break the news. "Sir, I…Sir, we've found two extra breakfast plates."

Angrily, King set the newspaper down on his desk and rubbed his temples. "I don't understand; what does that mean? You found two extra plates? Who made two extra plates?"

"It means, sir," the supervisor said with more confidence, "that two people are missing. We've searched every room, the bathrooms, the closets and even the administration wing and we can't find two people."

King could feel his blood boil. "Who's missing? Are they patients?"

"We don't know which two are missing but somehow, there are two extra portions for breakfast. We know exactly how many people should be here and two plates were not touched. Two patients must be missing or they're hiding and haven't eaten breakfast," said the supervisor, staring at her feet.

King got up from his desk, left his office, and exited through the steel doors. Staff members, including those in white, pink, blue, and green, were leading patients back to their rooms and it looked like organized confusion. The patients didn't understand why they were being brought back to their rooms and some didn't take this change in schedule well. To top it all off, many of the staff members didn't know who belonged to what room. Those in blue and green scrubs didn't know where to take people as they'd never had to deliver patients to their rooms before.

This was terribly upsetting for many patients. One overweight lady sat down at the breakfast table she recently vacated, crossed her arms over her chest, and refused to get up. Another man started banging on the table with his right fist and then his left. He refused to leave. Disturbing their routine caused confusion and agitation. Many patients hadn't had time to finish their breakfast and complained that they were still hungry. And they'd just left their rooms and didn't want to go back. Of course, an explanation would not have done much good, nor were any patients capable of understanding what was happening anyway. All they knew was this procedure was highly unusual, they didn't like it, and they were not inclined to cooperate.

Eventually, the common room was clear and the head nurse, Inez Lee, told Dr. King that Helen Parsons and Paige Whiteman were the two ladies missing. Their beds were empty and their blankets were missing.

"How did they get out?" King inquired, his face growing red.

"We don't know. The wooden door is locked," said Inez.

"And where is the key?" he demanded.

"I'll get it," said one of the other ladies in pink. She moved quickly toward the steel door, typed in the code, and returned seconds later. "It's gone. It's not hanging on its hook."

"When did they go?" asked King.

"Sometime after supper last night and before breakfast this morning," said Inez, shaking her head.

"Who was on duty last night?"

"Same as always. Andrea was in charge and Kenny was watching the monitors. When I came in this morning, we talked for a few minutes before they left. They said nothing about anyone missing," Nurse Lee said.

"I need to see the head of each section in my office... now," King boomed. "We need to get to the bottom of this. I want to know what happened."

Five minutes later the head nurse, the assistant nurse supervisor, the kitchen supervisor, and the cleaning supervisor met in King's office. He grilled them with questions until he was confident they had no idea of how the women escaped. Finally, he asked Inez Lee if she'd observed the behavior of the two women in question.

"Yes, since they were both relatively new, I observed them every day," said Inez, folding her hands in front of her pressed white skirt. "They had each slowed down as expected and seemed capable of sitting for long periods of time or just staring off into space. Honestly, I couldn't tell them apart from our older patients. They appeared to be adjusting and accepting they might be in the home for a while. Helen Parsons maybe hadn't accepted her situation completely, but in another week or two, she would have been right at home," the nurse continued.

Dr. King directed his attention to the supervisor in pink scrubs.

"I could see the gradual change that takes place and I would say both were right on schedule," she said. "That Helen Parsons was a feisty one at first and I didn't think the pill was working on her. Then about a week after she arrived, you could notice a change. It was like it was building up in her system."

Dr. King thought for a moment. "Do you think she was faking...making believe the pill was working?'

"I don't think so. I believe I would have noticed. We work with them every day and we know what to look for. Paige Whiteman has been acclimated for months now. There is no doubt with her. The pill was definitely doing its job," said the nurse in pink.

"Then how could those two get out of here?" King growled, pounding his fist on his desk. "If they were stoned like they should have been, they couldn't have found the key, opened the steel door, and gotten into the administration area. It's impossible unless they had help. And they had the gall to lock the door after they left. They even took the key."

"We think they used butter to lubricate the hinges on the front door so it would make less noise," said Inez.

King looked like he was about to have a stroke. "I want you all to get everyone you can to search along the highway. Search the grounds, the highways both north and south, any stores, and any houses five or six miles north and south of here. They couldn't have gone too far—I can't imagine they would know where to go. They might even be on the grounds. I want them found. Check if they're hiding in the woods. Bring them back. Go in groups of four."

"That doesn't leave many people here," said the kitchen supervisor.

"We'll survive. But if you don't bring those two ladies back, none of you will survive," King shouted.

CHAPTER FORTY-FOUR

Rather than return to the road, the two ladies stayed in the woods and walked south parallel to the road. Occasionally, they heard a car or truck on the road, but they were afraid it could be from the nursing home and didn't want to take the chance of being caught. They estimated the time as after six since the sun had not as yet risen.

"Paige, are you getting hungry?" Kathleen asked as they crunched their way through the fallen leaves.

"Sure am. That roll disappeared a long time ago and I'm thirsty."

"Let's see what we can find. I was hoping to come across a brook or small stream, but no luck."

"That's because we're on a ridge. Any stream or brook will be at the base of the hill. But it's much safer up here," said Paige. "See, I did learn something for my work with the girl scouts."

About a half hour later they could see a small brown log cabin nestled in a stand of pine trees. "I wonder if anyone lives there," said Paige. "It sure is small."

"Let's take a break and watch the house for a bit," Kathleen said as she slowed down. "Maybe we'll see a light or the owners will show themselves. How far do you think we walked?"

"We walked about two, maybe three hours and then another hour and a half after our nap. I'll bet we did at least ten miles...maybe eleven," Paige said, counting on her fingers. We didn't walk as fast in the woods as we did on the road.

"This house seems like a place where folks from the home might look since it's not far off the road," said Kathleen. "It might be smart to watch it for a bit."

Using their blankets as cushions, they sat behind a patch of mountain laurel and finished the last of their water. They didn't know the time, though the sun was now visible in the sky. Kathleen believed it was after seven but before eight. They were both hungry and thirsty.

About thirty minutes later, they were getting ready to approach the log cabin when a black SUV detoured off the road and started up the hill. The deciduous trees were bare of any foliage, but hiding behind the mountain laurel gave them some cover while still allowing them a good view of the car.

In a moment, four people dressed in green uniforms left the SUV and walked toward the front door of the house. The travelers quickly recognized them as kitchen staff from Lakeside Nursing Home. Two of the women went around the house and each looked through the window on a side of the house. The back of the log cabin had no window. The other two women stayed and banged on the front door. After several minutes, all four piled back into the SUV and headed back down the hill.

"Should we check it?" asked Paige.

"Might as well," said Kathleen. "No one seems to be home and I don't think anyone will be back for a while."

"I was hoping the owners would rescue us."

"No such luck," said Kathleen.

Cautiously, they approached the cabin, keeping the building between themselves and the road. They tried the front door but found it locked solid. "Let's look in the windows," Kathleen said. "I'll take the left and you the right." The two split up, leaving their blankets on the porch. Kathleen was looking in a window when she heard Paige yell. She ran around to the side of the house and saw Paige standing on a log, poised to put her leg through an open window.

"Give me a hand, Kathleen. I don't want to break anything." Kathleen helped Paige climb through the window. Paige said, "I'll open the front door. Meet you there."

The first order of business was to find some food. The refrigerator was bare except for staples like mustard, ketchup, salad dressing, and an unopened bottle of white wine. They also found a jar of marmalade.

"Kathleen, what I wouldn't give to sit down and enjoy that bottle of chardonnay. God, I sure miss a drink at dinner," said Paige.

"I did too. In fact, too much. I had to give up the booze a few years back," Kathleen said, opening a cabinet.

"Well, let's keep looking. Maybe we'll find some bread."

In the freezer, they found English muffins that had not been opened.

"Kathleen, we're in luck," Paige exclaimed. "We've got six muffins in the freezer and marmalade in the refrigerator. We're gonna have a party…or at least lunch."

"I think I found a pantry," said Kathleen. "Let's check it out."

The pantry didn't hold much, but there was a can of New England clam chowder and some canned vegetables. Kathleen also found some pasta and a jar of spaghetti sauce. "If the stove works, we can have a real lunch."

They found a pot, heated up the chowder and defrosted the muffins in the microwave. These were two women who were hungry. A half hour later they were satisfied and there was enough pasta for another meal.

"Paige," said Kathleen, rummaging through papers, "help me find the names of the people who own this place. Given the lack of fresh food, I'll bet this is their second home. If there's an envelope with their main address on it, we can send them some money and thank them for saving our lives. You check the end table by the bed and I'll look in the drawers in the kitchen."

Paige found an envelope with an address: Mr. and Mrs. William Lewis, 11207 County Road 205, Colombiana, Alabama. Kathleen tore the name off the envelope and put it in her coat pocket with the key from the nursing home. "I'll send them a check and a thank you note once we're safe," Kathleen said. "Now, what do we do?" Kathleen told Paige that the cabin was a good distance from Columbiana, so that address must be their permanent home.

CHAPTER FORTY-FIVE

*A*s each crew returned with the same discouraging news, Dr. King's speech grew more and more strident. He felt his staff's negligence was his biggest problem. He was loud and spoke quickly and slurred some of his words. "They must still be on the property," he said when the kitchen crew returned. "How far did you search?"

"We went ten miles south but couldn't turn around," said one of the ladies in green. "We had to drive another mile before we found a road. At the top of the road was a cabin but nobody was home. All four of us checked it out and it was completely empty. We could see the entire cabin."

"We've got to find them. They could be hurt," King said. But everyone knew he wasn't concerned about his patients' health or safety. He wanted them found to prevent the authorities from finding out he was housing several people who should not have been in his facility in the first place. He was afraid the police would find out about his scam. "Those two ladies must be found." That last sentence was emphatic.

When the meeting was over and the door to his office closed, King used a key to open the bottom drawer on the right of his desk. Inside sat a bottle of Jack Daniels and a glass resting on a towel. He took out the bottle and took a long pull on it, not bothering with the glass. He replaced the cap, put the bottle in the drawer, and locked it.

King seemed to take some comfort in the figures he was calculating. He was calculating the monthly profit results. He had trained his staff well and they never opened the door to his office without knocking and waiting for him to say 'enter.' If he didn't tell them to come in, they were not to enter. Termination, he promised, would be the consequence other wise.

As the women in green returned to the kitchen, one whispered to the other, "I believe our boss has decided on a liquid lunch. If my nose is not playing tricks on me."

It was now time for lunch. The staff still needed to retrieve patients from their rooms and set out the utensils, drinks, and sandwiches, so it was all hands on deck. Even the nurses were pressed into making sandwiches since time had been taken from the kitchen crew.

After the staff had served lunch and the dishes put away, King called his people together. "I don't think they could have walked ten miles," he said. "That would be too much for ladies this age to walk. In fact, they are probably only a short distance from here. Drive ten miles from the home, turn around and work your way back. Ask at any service station; stop at every home, store, and building. Look for signs of forced entry. They couldn't have gotten too far. They are without proper clothes, food, or water. And besides, they're old. Paige is sixty-five and Kathleen...excuse me...Helen Parsons is almost sixty-eight.

Inez and Maggie eyed each other at the mention of 'Kathleen.' Now, there was no doubt. They knew King's secret and were convinced he was a criminal.

"I'll bet they got a ride in a car," a big lady from the cleaning group offered by way of explanation. "Someone just happened to drive by and stopped for them. That's what happened."

"That's not what happened," King insisted. He had become domineering and was not open to reason. "No one would give two old people outside a crazy house a ride in the middle of the night—or in the morning, for that matter. No one in his or her right mind. And none of you saw them on the road when you were coming to work. Drive ten miles and have one group take one side of the road and the other take the other side. Hurry! They can't get away." He cleared his throat then added, "They need to be rescued or they will die out there."

The same kitchen crew went south, as did two nurses and two assistant nurses in a caravan of two cars. The cleaning crew and other nurses went north. When the odometer said ten miles, they looked for a place to turn around and as previously, couldn't find one. The road was too narrow and had too many turns to safely reverse their direction. They continued driving until they reached eleven miles and the same log cabin they had previously searched. Both cars pulled into the driveway, one behind the other.

The kitchen crew in the black SUV wanted to back out, but the nurses were behind them, planning to drive up the road and check out the log cabin.

"What they trying to do?" said the driver of the SUV. She signaled for them to turn around and go back, but they weren't moving. She gestured four or five times for the car in the rear to back out, but they refused. Finally, angry because they weren't moving, she got out to give the nurse a piece of her mind.

"Back your car up and get the hell out of my way," said the woman in green.

"We're gonna check out that log cabin," said the nurse in white.

"Hell, you are! We done checked it out this morning and nothin's there. All four of us. No sense checking it again," she said.

"Well, we're gonna check it out for ourselves," the nurse insisted. "Besides, this is our side of the street."

Now this was no longer a discussion of who was going to do what. It had just become personal. *That bitch is not gonna talk to me that way,* thought the kitchen staffer. *Those damn nurses think they can boss us and tell us what to do, but they have no authority out here on the road. We'll do what we damn well please.*

"We're looking on this side of the street. You can have the other side," said the woman in green.

"Who are you to tell us where we can search?" said the nurse in white.

"This is the eleven-mile mark and we're supposed to stop at ten miles. You're gonna lose this argument with me and with Dr. King. I'll see he fires your ass. Now back that car up, go back a mile, and search on that side of the street." The kitchen supervisor smiled, pleased to finally have a chance to assert herself to the almighty nurses. They were away from the home and this was an even playing field.

"Those nurses be damned," the kitchen supervisor said to her crew. "This is one argument they're not going to win. She can't outsmart me." Besides those who worked in the kitchen were bigger. Several nurses in white had made that observation.

A second nurse joined the discussion. "Come on, Darlene, you're not gonna win an argument with that bitch. Every minute we sit here is that much later we go home. What does it matter what side of the street we search? We're never gonna find them two."

The nurses finally relented and backed onto the road, heading back toward the nursing home. Once the nurses had gone, the ladies in green followed. They looked at the odometer and drove exactly a mile before beginning their search. They drove slowly, looking for any disturbance in the grass by the side of the road or any house, store, or building in the woods. They knew it would be about an hour before they'd return to the nursing home, and they had little expectation they'd be successful in their quest. The disagreement with the nurses was soon forgotten.

CHAPTER FORTY-SIX

"This is a cute little bungalow," said Paige, taking a seat by a window.

"I'm glad we found it and you found that window open," Kathleen replied.

"It's nice to rest here and plan our next move."

"I'm happy to stay here until we can find a better place or find some way to get a phone," Kathleen said, continuing to explore the kitchen.

"You know, Kathleen, we could make that food last for another few days," Paige said. "There's quite a bit of spaghetti and sauce and plenty of water. All we need to do is turn on the faucet."

"And you're just dying to open that bottle of wine," Kathleen chided.

"You bet your ass, I am," Paige said with a genuine laugh that Kathleen was delighted to hear. "It's been a while since I had wine with my meal and I'm going to enjoy a glass."

"Do you think anyone will be back here soon?" Kathleen asked, watching the door.

"Those ladies in green already searched the cabin. They saw the place was empty and it may be a day or two before they try again. I'm sure we'll be safe overnight."

"Maybe the owners will pay us a visit and take us back to civilization and the authorities," Kathleen said, as she looked through the kitchen drawers.

"We just don't want anyone taking us back to Lakeside," said Paige and Kathleen nodded her approval.

Kathleen stood with her back to the front door and looked around the cabin. The kitchen was to the right and had an electric stove, a sink, and a microwave. A refrigerator faced toward the center of the cabin. To her left was a round table with two wooden chairs and a half bath was to the left and against the back wall. A bed occupied the space on the rear wall, windows were on each side of the door, and there was a window on each side of the house. There were no windows in the back of the cabin. The cabin would be a nice weekend retreat for two people who wanted to spend time with each other.

It was at that moment they heard the sound of a vehicle coming up the driveway. "Oh, shit," said Kathleen, stepping away from the window.

"Damn," said Paige as she looked out the corner of the window, careful not to be seen. "Two cars are parked about half way up the hill in the driveway. One looks like the SUV that those kitchen people were driving. Now what are they doing coming back?"

"Let's hide our blankets and put the dishes in the sink," said Kathleen, grabbing the plates. "If we hide under the bed, they won't see us. Did you lock that bedroom window?"

"It's locked." The car in the rear honked four times. "Look, those cars aren't moving, just sitting there. The lady in green is yelling at the nurses to back up. Now she's getting out of the car. She's ready for a fight." Paige continued to narrate as Kathleen hastily tidied up the kitchen, then after a moment, she added, "There they go...they're on the road and going back toward the home."

"Thank goodness," said Kathleen. "Paige, we're safe here at least for a day or so. Time is on our side. The home will have to notify the police or they could be in serious trouble. The administrator can't expect thirty people, or however many employees they have, to keep quiet about all of this. That's asking too much."

"I guess we're safe, then," said Paige. "I don't suppose they'll look here again, at least not today. And they can't scour the woods on a daily basis. We have food and a bed and we can warm the house with the stove. Let's stay. Tomorrow we can decide what to do."

"And besides, you have a bottle of wine that needs to be finished."

"Kathleen, I'm glad you understand," said Paige with a smile. It felt good to smile again.

The two women were able to take a nap after lunch that lasted several hours. The previous night was long and strenuous; their journey was filled with fear and emotion and had been extremely taxing for two people in their sixties.

They curled up on the bed and covered themselves with the blankets from the home. It was four thirty by the clock in the kitchen when they started moving about in the diminishing sunlight. In a half hour or so, it would be dark.

"Kathleen, if you have no objection, I'm going to open that bottle of Chardonnay," said Paige.

"Why should I object? Hell, if I wasn't on the wagon, I'd join you. Mind if I toast with a glass of water?" asked Kathleen.

"That would be nice. We'll have our own happy hour," said Paige.

"Do we dare turn on the lights?" Kathleen asked.

"Maybe if we could darken the windows," Paige mused, walking toward the kitchen. "I saw some thumb tacks in one of the drawers and there are newspapers in the pantry."

"You get the thumbtacks and I'll find the paper. Then we can turn on the lamp."

It wasn't but a few minutes later that the windows were covered. The light wasn't completely unseen from outside, so the two got bath towels and hung them over the curtain rods to add extra heft to the curtains. That did it.

Paige found a pot under the stove. She filled it half full of water, turned on the stove, and brought out the spaghetti from the pantry closet. Kathleen got out the dishes and set the table. Paige then found a bottle opener and set about opening the bottle of wine.

Kathleen found a wine glass and filled a second wine glass with water for herself.

When the wine was poured, Kathleen said, "To meeting such a wonderful person in such a terrible place. Thank you for being my roommate and keeping me from turning into a zombie."

"And thank you, Kathleen, for getting that key and getting us out of that god-awful place," said Paige. "To our future, whatever that might be. God willing, it will be happy."

They clinked glasses and sat down at the kitchen table.

"Ups," said Kathleen. As she sat down, the key in her pocket pressed against her stomach. "If it wasn't for the big key, we would still be locked up in that miserable place." Kathleen took the key out of her pocket and placed it in the center of the table, resting against the wine bottle. "To the key." She raised her glass of water.

"Thanks to the key. I look forward to using it to open that door and arrest those suckers...If not us, then the authorities."

When they finished their pasta dinner, Paige asked Kathleen to tell her something about herself. "I know you had one child and he died several years ago," said Paige. "He married Carol and had two children until Tillie came along and he divorced Carol. What else can you tell me?"

"My husband, Joseph, was in the navy during Vietnam," said Kathleen. "He served on an aircraft carrier off shore. We only had the one child. I couldn't have any more, but I was happy with one. So was my husband. He died of a heart attack at age forty. His son also died young. Neither had good health. My son, being a diabetic, was not faithful to his diet when he was married to Carol. His poor health continued when he lived with Tillie.

"I miss both my men, but I've learned to live alone," she continued. "George and Carol had two children, Paul and Patti, and I have three grandchildren. As you know, I don't see them very often since they live in Anniston and Pell City. I've been a crossing guard for the past twenty years and I'm going to miss it now I'm retired. How about you? Tell me your story."

"Mine's not so complicated," said Paige, sipping at her wine. "I always wanted to be a nurse. I was in college, half way through my schooling, when I married Charles. He had two years of college but one day he came home and told me he'd enlisted in the marines. He was shipped to Vietnam and several months later I was told he was attacked in an ambush north of Saigon and was blown up. There was no body to be shipped home. I'm not sure he knew that I was pregnant unless he received the last letter I sent him. He left me with a daughter and a big hole in my life. I finished my schooling, worked as a nurse, became head nurse in the operating room, and worked for over thirty years in hospitals. During that time, I bought a small house in Vestavia, raised my daughter, planted a vegetable garden, and did a lot of cooking. I went to concerts, plays, and recitals, and I volunteered to help children learn to read. My daughter did everything in her power to make my life miserable. That included the day she drugged me and put me in that miserable, evil Lakeside Nursing Home."

"I'm sorry, Paige," said Kathleen, placing a hand on her shoulder. "Living with someone who doesn't love you is a terrible burden. Thanks for sharing your story."

"And for sharing yours," said Paige. "I'm glad I was able to tell that to somebody."

CHAPTER FORTY-SEVEN

*A*nthony Robertson hadn't gone back to the jail after his meeting with the prosecutor. He never liked going to the jail under the best of circumstances and dealing with this client taxed his patience. He seldom liked any of the clients assigned to him, but knew he had to take what was given to him since he was starting his practice. But Tillie Larson was different. He would fight for her and represent her to the best of his ability, but he didn't have to like it. And he didn't have to like her.

He waited a day before he returned to the jail and in the middle of the afternoon he asked to see his client.

A guard escorted him to the visitor's room where he waited for his client. The visitor's room contained a long table with a chair on each side. The room was painted cream and had just the one door. A small two-way mirror hung on the way next to the door. After about five minutes, a guard escorted Tillie in.

"Well, what did he say?" asked Tillie, avoiding eye contact.

"You're not going to like what he said. So don't kill the messenger."

"Get on with it," Tillie demanded.

"He said the best offer you're going to get is five years in prison with five years' probation. That is, if Mrs. Larson is found safe and healthy, you restore any money you have stolen, and you behave yourself in prison."

"I can't accept that," said Tillie, rolling her eyes. She put her head in her hands and mumbled, "I guess they want to see the lady die. Well, if that's what they want, that's what they'll get."

"I should add, it's my personal advice that you will not get a better deal. If you wait another day to come forward or if the authorities find Ms. Larson on their own, you are looking at twenty to life. The prosecuting attorney wanted me to know his patience is short and if you don't accept this offer, it will be withdrawn." The last comment voiced Anthony's own thoughts rather than what the prosecuting attorney had actually said. He did think those were the prosecuting attorney's sentiments, however. He also believed five years in the slammer was lenient. It was Anthony's firm belief that Tillie should take the offer since she was not going to get anything better.

"I'm not gonna spend any five years in jail. Tell them I won't take it. Let the lady die," Tillie said, folding her arms.

"I'll tell them. I understand you want to spend the rest of your life in prison, but I'm advising you against rejecting this plea bargain. You don't seem to understand what kind of serious trouble you've gotten yourself into. I'll tell them, but I want you to understand you are making a very big mistake," said Anthony as he walked toward the door and called the guard.

Paige only drank two glasses of wine, but those two glasses made her tipsy. She put the cork back in the bottle and returned it to the refrigerator.

"Kathleen, I'm feeling the effects of the wine and I want to go to bed," she said. "It sure was nice to have a glass of wine. I feel so relaxed. It's been so long since I last had any alcohol, it almost wiped me out. Would you mind if I go to bed?"

"Not at all. You haven't had much to eat. That means there wasn't much food to absorb that alcohol. I'll join you. I think it will be okay to sleep on the top of the bed using our blankets. I'll use one of their pillows, though," said Kathleen.

"What time do you think it is?"

"The kitchen clock says five minutes past seven. Based on when the sun went down, I'd say that's correct. I didn't have wine, but I'm ready for bed, too. We don't know what tomorrow will bring, but at least we'll be rested if we go to bed now."

"And I like the hotel we picked," Paige said with a grin. "Let's get ready for bed."

The two brushed their teeth with toothpaste they found in the bathroom, using their fingers as toothbrushes. They slept in their clothes. The two blankets they brought from the nursing home were sufficient to keep them warm and they were both asleep within five minutes.

CHAPTER FORTY-EIGHT

"Aren't we going to call the police?" Inez Lee stood up and voiced her opinion even before Dr. King had called the staff meeting to order. "If we don't call the police, we could be charged with some serious violations of our responsibilities. We need to call the police," she insisted. Inez sounded confident, but she had no idea how King would react to her sympathy for the patients.

King had called this extraordinary meeting of his supervisors immediately after breakfast on the day following Paige and 'Helen's' disappearance. It was their usual meeting time, but they'd already had a staff meeting this week. King was concerned some of his staff might get out of line and call the authorities without permission. He couldn't allow that and he wanted to know if he was going to have trouble with anybody. He was surprised his head nurse started speaking before he'd called the meeting to order.

"We need to call the po—" was as far as she got when King's voice interrupted her.

"There is no need to call the authorities," he snapped. "Once we find those two, there will be a logical explanation. We haven't considered the possibility that someone came for them. The...." "At midnight or two in the morning?" asked the big woman in charge of the kitchen. "Who would come for them at that time of night? That doesn't make sense." Several staff members nodded their agreement as she continued, "If anyone was coming for them, it would be in daylight. No, they escaped! We could all be in serious trouble if we don't notify the authorities."

"No one is going to notify the authorities," King said, raising his voice. "Paige and Helen are perfectly safe, I can tell you that. They wouldn't have tried to sneak out of here at night if they didn't have anywhere to go. For all we know, they may be on the grounds or a mile or two away from here, hiding in the bushes. When they get hungry, they'll come out," he said, trying to regain his composure

"Dr. King, that's nonsense!" Inez stood up and pointed to the huge door and the windows with bars on them. "This place is locked up tighter than a prison. There are no phones except the one in your office and our patients have no one to contact even if they wanted to call. The patients are all on medication and even if they were physically capable, they wouldn't be mentally capable of removing themselves from this facility. Even if they had a phone to call for someone, no one would be able to enter this building. It's time to contact the police; otherwise we'll all go to jail."

Inez paused to judge the others' agreement and a few other staff members nodded. Then, just when everyone believed she was about to sit down, she continued to speak, "Those two ladies walked out of here on purpose. They weren't rescued or forced to leave. They left because they wanted to leave. They locked that big ol' door with the key to tell us they didn't want to come back. No, sir. They left because they didn't want to live here anymore. And you know what else? I don't think they were suffering from mental disease at all." Inez spoke with conviction as several staff members whispered between themselves. "They were two ladies in their sixties, not suffering from dementia, and we were treating them as if they had lost their damn minds."

King stood up from behind his desk and all knew he was not going to agree. Many in the room wondered why he'd allowed the discussion to go on for this long. Inez suspected he wanted to know who he could trust and who might betray him.

"Listen to me and listen to me carefully," he said. "No one is going to contact the authorities. If anyone does, I will have their job. If one of your staff members calls, she will lose her job as well as you. If anyone is going to call the authorities, it will be me. We will find Mrs. Whiteman and Mrs….ah…Parsons…in the next day or two and they will be perfectly healthy. They wouldn't leave here to go to someplace where it was cold and dangerous. No one will call the police. Do you hear me? Nurse Lee, you are on very shaky ground if you think those two ladies weren't crazy. Since when did you become a doctor?" He paused as Inez lowered her gaze to the floor. "If anyone is planning to call the authorities, tell me now and I will arrange to have your check sent to you."

King waited until he got an answer or at least a nod from each of the supervisors. He then continued. "Go back to your stations and tell your people they will not contact the authorities. If they do, they will forfeit their job. I want two from cleaning and two from nursing to go out this morning and two from the other groups to go out this afternoon. One car will go north and the other south. Discretely ask at the gas stations and stores. Tell them you are looking for your mother who sometimes wanders away from the house. Call me if you find anything. Now is *not* the time for the police."

Inez Lee, as the head nurse and a woman who always displayed compassion, determined that no matter the outcome, she would be the one to take the fall if these two ladies were found or if they weren't. Supposedly, Dr. King was bound by the Hippocratic Oath, but Nurse Lee rightly surmised he didn't take the oath seriously. *Perhaps he isn't even a real doctor,* she thought. If that were the case, Inez would be the only person bound to caring for the patients, legally that is. She had taken the Florence Nightingale Pledge to never harm those entrusted to her care and her conscience was telling her someone needed to be notified or these women would die. She wondered if perhaps it was too late.

Inez was genuinely concerned about those entrusted to her and many times had resolved to quit. *If I do quit, though,* she thought, *who will support my daughters? Who else will hire me if I get fired?* Unemployment was high and if she turned Dr. King in, who would speak on her behalf? She needed to consider these things, but wondered how much longer she could live with herself if she didn't notify someone, if for no other reason than self-protection. Maybe she would call someone today.

CHAPTER FORTY-NINE

*C*arol could stand it no longer. She called Rudy who assured her the police were doing all they could. What more could anyone do? She walked around the office, made herself some tea, and still could find no satisfaction. She was missing something. She called Drew.

"Drew? Carol here. I can't get it out of my head that we're not doing all we can to find Kathleen. What did you find out about the visit to the notary? Surely, she must know something?"

"Hey, Carol," said Drew. "I spoke with the detective who interviewed Janice, the notary, and she insists all she did wrong was swear she witnessed a signature she didn't actually witness. She did that because she trusted Tillie—they're friends. But she also admitted she was afraid of Tillie. The detective said it was up to the prosecuting attorney to take it from there, have her license withdrawn, and indict her for perjury."

"That may make them feel good, but it doesn't tell us where Tillie's hidden Kathleen or if she's okay."

"What do you suggest we do?" Drew asked, rubbing his temples.

"I recommend you and I visit that notary at the insurance company and try to find out where Kathleen could be," Carol suggested. "That Janice must know what kinds of projects Tillie was working on and maybe that will give us a clue. We have some leverage with Janice. If Kathleen were to be harmed or hurt, she would bear a lot of the responsibility. Maybe a little threatening will get her thinking about where Kathleen could possibly be. Tillie's supervisor might also be of help. Tillie didn't do this on the spur of the moment. It was well planned and Janice Hoffman or her supervisor might have some information." Carol paced as she spoke, it always helped her to think.

"I'll bet you're right," said Drew. "The police were only looking at it from the legal angle. We need to find out if Tillie was connected to any nursing home. Maybe she provided insurance to a nursing home and had some control over people who worked there."

"Right," Carol said. "I think it would be wise to find out what kind of work she was doing. The police didn't find anything, so maybe we can try. I'll call the insurance company and see if we can schedule a meeting with them."

"Carol, why don't we just visit them...take them by surprise? We can't let these folks talk to each other to coordinate their stories, if they were so inclined. When are you free?" Drew asked.

"How about now. Pick me up at my office. I'll be free in fifteen minutes," Carol said.

"I'm on my way," said Drew, grabbing his coat from a hook behind his desk. "I'll meet you in the parking lot by the front door. See you then."

Drew drove Carol to the Apex Insurance Company offices on Lakeshore Parkway and asked to see Anna Mae Glass. Anna Mae led them into her office and took a seat at her desk, seeming surprisingly calm.

"Have you found Mrs. Larson yet?" She asked. "I'm anxious to help in any way possible." She seemed genuinely interested in solving this problem.

"Not yet. That's why we're here," said Drew. "Do you have any idea where she might be? If she were by herself or decided to visit a friend, we believe she would have contacted Carol. She hasn't done that. Someone must be housing her, feeding her, and keeping her alive."

"That could be any number of retirement homes or nursing homes. Have you tried calling nursing homes?" Anna Mae offered.

"We've called them all within a fifty miles radius and no home has a Kathleen Larson on their records," Drew said, shaking his head. "We keep coming up empty, yet we feel certain Tillie would have made some provision to house Ms. Larson.. We don't believe she's the type to take her mother-in-law for a ride, hit her with a shovel, and bury her in a shallow grave." At this, Anna Mae sat upright, clearly growing more uncomfortable.

"Tillie has said unless we dismiss the charges against her, she won't tell us where Kathleen is being kept,"

Drew continued. "That's why we believe she has made arrangements."

"I'm sorry I can't be of help," Anna Mae said as she rose from her chair, ready to dismiss her visitors. It was obvious she was uncomfortable with the tone and direction of the conversation.

"Mrs. Glass," said Carol, not making a move to relinquish her chair, "what kind of work did Tillie do?"

"The same kind of work we all do," Anna Mae answered. "We provide medical insurance to doctors, hospitals, retirement and nursing homes, and we monitor the social security checks they receive to prevent fraud. I thought you understood that."

"Did Tillie deal with nursing homes?" Carol asked.

"Yes, she oversaw the largest share of our nursing home business. And I might add, she was very good about keeping them in line. She made sure they didn't get away with cheating us," Anna Mae said with a smile.

"How would they cheat you?" asked Carol.

"Sometimes nursing homes are lax in telling us when a person dies in order to collect another month or two of social security payments. Tillie stayed on top of that. She wouldn't hesitate to call them on it and saw to it that they returned any overpayments."

Drew spoke up. "Mrs. Glass, would it be possible to see a list of the nursing homes Tillie dealt with? It's possible one of those homes is harboring Mrs. Larson."

"I believe we split Tillie's work with several of our agents. Let me see who's doing that work." Anna Mae got up and went to her files. "Yes, we split the work between Janice Hoffman and Marie Carroll. Janice is the notary who assisted Tillie in forging the power of attorney document," she added, matter-of-factly.

"And you kept her in your employment?" Carol snapped.

"They did take away her license to be a notary."

"May we speak with her, first…alone?" asked Drew.

"I'll get her," said Anna Mae.

It was now almost four-thirty in the afternoon. The shadows along the wall were growing longer and Carol wondered where her mother-in-law could be. She said a prayer for her safe return.

CHAPTER FIFTY

"Janice, you do know you're in a lot of trouble, correct?" Drew began.

"I don't see why. They took away my notary license," Janice groaned.

"Yes, that's the least of your problems. You may yet be charged with perjury or a felony as an accessory to a crime," Drew threatened. "Mrs. Larson is still missing and Tillie refuses to tell us where she is. If she dies or is injured, you will be charged in that crime as an accessory, along with Tillie. You assisted her in stealing from Mrs. Larson. You were also instrumental in getting Tillie the POA. Right now, we're only interested in seeing Kathleen Larson safe and sound and back in her own home. If that doesn't happen, charges *will* be filed. In addition to the perjury charges, you're looking at several other felonies. You may be looking at a long time in prison." The veins in Drew's forehead bulged as he spoke, revealing agitation in what was usually his calm and quiet demeanor.

"I didn't know what she was about to do..." Janice pleaded.

"Yet you performed a criminal act that might lead to death or at least of depriving a person of all their rights," Drew added.

"I had no intention of harming Mrs. Larson," Janice said sternly. "Tillie is just impossible to say 'no' to. She doesn't take rejection easily and I couldn't say no to her. I thought she was my friend. I didn't know she would involve me in this kind of trouble. I trusted her."

"So, you trusted her not to get you in trouble?" Carol asked.

"If I had known what she was about to do, I wouldn't have helped her," said Janice.

Drew decided to take a different approach. "Tell me Janice, did Tillie work with many nursing homes?"

"Yes. I'm presently working with most of the homes she supervised," Janice said, happy for a change of subject.

"Are there any that are isolated or very restrictive?" asked Drew.

"You mean, like don't have visitors or restrict use of phones? Like that?"

"Yes, that's what I'm looking for. Do you supervise any like that?" he asked.

"Yes, we have three or four that are for those who are mentally ill. They are usually out in the country, house people with Alzheimer's or severe dementia and keep the patients confined. They are housed, fed, and not allowed to harm each other. We provide insurance for those homes as well as for assisted living and retirement communities," said Janice.

"Could you give me the names and addresses of those restrictive facilities?" Drew requested.

"I'll ask Mrs. Glass," Janice replied. "I'll need her permission before I can give you that information."

She returned moments later with Anna Mae who nodded as she spoke. "We'll be happy to provide you with whatever you request. We hope it will lead to finding Mrs. Larson. Janice can help you."

Janice showed them a list of those nursing homes that paid insurance premiums. Most were in Birmingham and were recognized as reputable businesses. These were not all the facilities that provided services, but rather those that bought their insurance from Apex. It was easy to eliminate all the assisted living or open retirement communities as Kathleen would surely have contacted someone if she were living there.

The four most restrictive facilities that housed the mentally ill were outside the metropolitan area. Carol estimated they were each at least thirty minutes away from downtown Birmingham.

"Did Tillie visit any of these facilities recently?" Carol didn't know why she asked this question. The thought just popped into her head. She was glad it did.

"She may have," said Anna Mae. "About a month ago, possibly two, she told me she was going to Shelby County to visit a home. She didn't say which one or why she was going there. That would eliminate the two facilities that are in Jefferson County. That leaves us with Lakeside near Columbiana and Pine Forest near Montevallo. I'd put my money on Lakeside since it's out in the country and quite isolated."

"Would you please give me the addresses of both of those facilities?" Carol asked. "We would like to visit them. The phone numbers, also. Please don't contact them for the next few days."

"Of course not," said Anna Mae. "Call me if I can be of any further help. I would like to know if you locate Mrs. Larson," she added as she rose from her chair and extended her hand.

"I would feel terrible if anything happened to that lady because of my stupidity," Janice said. "I am truly sorry. You have to understand Tillie gets what she wants. She doesn't take 'no' for an answer."

"Let's hope we find her for your sake as well as Mrs. Larson's. Janice, you've been very helpful," said Carol. "I'll try to put in a good word about you helping us find Kathleen...if we should be so lucky."

Drew and Carol left and immediately contacted the police. The detective who had interviewed Janice the day before didn't seem to put any value on the information given to him.

"It's helpless," said the detective. "Tillie will have to tell us where Ms. Kathleen is being kept. There are just too many homes to investigate," he said.

"Drew, I'll take off from work tomorrow," said Carol as they walked back to his car. "If we use the

GPS, we should be able to find Lakeside first and then Pine Forest."

"It's worth a try. I'll call you in the morning," he said, and they shook on it.

CHAPTER FIFTY-ONE

Paige and Kathleen were awake as the gray light of dawn peeked through the paper on the windows. The first thing Paige did was take down the window coverings to allow daylight to fill the room. She announced the time as six-thirty, as was the time on the kitchen clock.

Kathleen made some coffee first and then poured two bowls of cereal. They had to eat it dry since there was no milk in the refrigerator. They weren't particularly anxious to leave the warmth and comfort of the log cabin for the unknown, but they went about the tasks necessary to prepare themselves. Paige found another plastic container, which they filled with water and they decided to take their blankets with them since those were their only possessions besides the clothes on their backs. Neither knew what was in store for them.

Around nine o'clock, they could think of no other reason to stay. They had cleaned up the cabin, leaving it the way they found it, and it didn't look as if anybody had inhabited the place recently. They put whatever trash they made in a plastic bag, sealed it, and placed it in the cabinet under the sink.

"The window wasn't locked when we got here, so it's best we leave it the way we found it," Paige said.

"I agree," said Kathleen. "We should leave it the way we found it. If the people from Lakeside come to investigate again, it's best if they see it the way we found it the first time."

Both ladies left by way of the front door, allowing the door to lock when they closed it. Then, looking like medieval characters in an Emily Bronte novel, the two ladies moved through the woods along the high ridge that ran parallel to the road. The weather was in the mid-fifties and a bit cloudy. There wasn't much traffic, but the two travelers were reluctant to take a chance on being discovered by people from Lakeside Nursing Home. Anyone else who saw them would think they were crazy and would report them to the home or the police, or drive them to the home itself. Neither outcome was acceptable.

After they had gone about two miles without encountering so much as a home, they sat on their blankets and took a break.

"Kathleen, we do pretty good for two old broads," Paige said, catching her breath.

"We do, but we're gonna pay for it in the morning. Walking on trails would be easier," said Kathleen, "and there are no trails up here. I feel it in my hips and knees."

"Now that you mention it, so do I," said Paige. "I hope we find a cabin or home soon so we can call someone. I'd settle for a restaurant or convenience store where we could tell them our story and ask them to contact the Homewood Police."

"My daughter-in-law, Carol, must be out of her mind," Kathleen said. "I know she's looking for us. If only we could get to a phone."

After a twenty-minute rest, Paige struggled to her feet and extended her hand to assist Kathleen. They continued on their journey. It was only about ten minutes later when Kathleen let out a yell that scared Paige. "Son-of-a-bitch!" she screamed.

"Kathleen...what happened?" Paige said, scurrying ahead to meet her.

"I stepped into a hole and twisted my ankle," Kathleen groaned. "Damn, that hurts! Shit, this is gonna slow us. Oh, I'm so sorry, Paige."

"It's not your fault," Paige said. "Sit down on your blanket and let's have a look at that ankle."

Paige had long since retired from active nursing, but you couldn't take the training out of someone so dedicated. She removed Kathleen's shoe and examined the ankle. "Does that hurt?" she asked as she probed her left ankle. Kathleen nodded. "You've sprained your ankle, all right. I don't believe you broke it. You would have yelled a lot louder if you had. Let's get your foot back in your shoe before it swells up."

"Oh, Paige, I'm so sorry. We didn't need this to happen," Kathleen said, wiggling her shoe onto her foot.

"Well, it could have been worse. You could have broken your leg again."

"You're right, I should be grateful I didn't. What should we do now?" Kathleen asked.

"I know it won't be easy, but if we make it back to the log cabin, we can survive," said Paige. "We know where that is and we have no idea what lies ahead of us. Can you make it back to the cabin?"

"I think so. It would help if I had a walking stick," said Kathleen. "Look for a stick we can use. I know we'll find something."

With Kathleen putting some of her weight on Paige's arm, they moved north toward the cabin at about half the speed they were traveling before. The women could easily see the tracks they'd made in the dirt and leaves on their trip south.

Kathleen saw a long straight branch leaning against a live oak tree and Paige retrieved it and gave it to her. It was a bit too long and would have been ideal if it were a foot shorter. Paige tried to break it over her knee, but with little success. She found a log nearby that was the right size and placed the branch on it, adjusting it so she wouldn't break off too much. Then, with a smart stomp of her heel, she broke the branch off in exactly the right place.

"You'll make a good girl scout, one of these days," Kathleen said.

Paige laughed. "Don't make fun of my skills in the woods. In my younger days, I was a den mother for my daughter's brownie troop. You'll never know when you might use some skills you thought were long forgotten."

This brought back conversation about their lives and their roles as wives and mothers, their jobs and hobbies, and their husbands. All the while they moved closer to the cabin, retracing their steps along the way.

CHAPTER FIFTY-TWO

*D*r. King told Inez Lee to take Maggie Pope with her to patrol the road to the south. He was not aware these two women were friends and carpooled daily to work. In fact, there was a lot about his staff Dr. King didn't know. It was almost nine in the morning and Inez was interested to know what her fellow staff member thought about their current situation. Maggie hadn't said anything one way or the other and gave no indication as to whether she could be trusted with what Inez wanted to do.

"Maggie, what do you think of us having to search the woods for two patients?" This was the most open inquiry Inez could think of at the time. She wanted Maggie to tell her what she really was thinking, rather than trying to solicit an answer.

"It's not what I thought I'd be doing when I took this job," Maggie said, biting her lip.

"What did you expect?" Inez asked.

"I thought we'd be taking blood pressure, moving the patients to therapy, bathing them, and talking with them. Instead they talk to themselves, have no physical problems the staff is actually concerned with, and they receive absolutely no stimulation. Since they do nothing, weekly showers are really all they need. What a horrible existence," Maggie said, shaking her head.

"I agree and I don't like the situation we've found ourselves in, being asked to round up two patients who fled into the woods in the middle of the night," said Inez.

"I hope they don't come back to the home. There's no one walking on the road and I don't see any homes in the area," said Maggie.

"There's that log cabin at the eleven-mile marker. We can check that out. It's really the only place around here that could house someone. I wanted to visit that cabin the other day, but the four ladies from the kitchen turned around in the driveway and wouldn't let us go up the hill. They said they had checked it out that morning and it was empty," said Inez. "But who knows."

"If you want to check it out, let's do it. I don't see the harm and besides, it's the only place south of the home that would provide shelter," said Maggie.

"I don't see how they could get that far on foot," Inez said, shaking her head. "I think it's impossible for two patients to do that in the middle of the night." After a moment she added, "Let's check it anyway."

The two ladies drove up the highway until they reached the cabin. It had a circular driveway in front that allowed them to turn the car to face down the hill. Inez parked the car and put on the emergency brake. Then the two walked to the cottage.

"It's cute," said Maggie.

"And small."

Each looked in a front window, then Maggie tried the door and found it locked.

"Let's look in the side windows," she said.

They looked through the north-facing window and saw the dining area and some of the kitchen. "It doesn't look like it's been used in a while. Sure is neat," said Maggie.

Then the nurses walked around back where there were no windows and continued until they came to the south window. "Hey, look. That window is open," Maggie said.

"The kitchen ladies didn't say anything about the window," said Inez. "They probably didn't even notice. It's best we leave it alone."

The two walked around front and decided they had wasted enough time.

"It's a shame those two old ladies didn't find this cabin. It would have kept them warm and safe," said Inez.

"Girl…" said Maggie. "Do you think they're dead?"

"I'm not sure *we* could have survived a night in the woods if we didn't have a shelter of sorts. And we're young. They're old and not in the best of shape. I don't know who's gonna search these woods, but there's a whole lot of woods to search. My best guess is a year from now a dog or some hikers will find their bones under a pile of leaves," said Inez with a shiver. "Maggie, let's get out of here. This talk of finding dead bodies is giving me the creeps."

The two drove back to Lakeside. As they walked toward the back entrance, Inez said, "Maggie, come with me to report to Dr. King. He'll believe us if we both tell him the same thing. I think he's paranoid sometimes and isn't inclined to believe what people tell him."

"Yeah, I know what you mean," said Maggie. "No matter what I tell him, I get the feeling he's not buying. I think that's because he lies all the time and thinks other people do it, too."

"I know, girl," said Inez. "All I know is he doesn't trust what you tell him. Having two people tell him the same thing might help."

They knocked on the door to Dr. King's office.

"Come in," he said.

"We just returned from the south," said Inez.

"Did you go ten miles?"

"We stopped at that small log cabin at the eleven-mile marker," she said. "That's the only place to turn around. We stopped there yesterday and we looked in the windows again today. It was exactly the same."

"Nobody's been there," said Maggie.

"Are you sure?" King insisted.

"I am," Inez spoke up. "Nothing was out of place. We looked through the windows and no one was there. You can see the entire inside. Nothing was disturbed."

"Okay. I'll take your word for it. And you didn't see anything along the road on the way back to here?" King asked.

"No," Maggie interjected. "We especially watched the bushes to see if anyone went into the woods from the road. I checked it out while Inez drove. There are drainage ditches on both sides of the road. They would have left a mess walking through those ditches, but we ain't seen any sign of them. No, sir."

"Well, I'm sorry we haven't found them," King said, running his hands through his hair. "I don't want to see them hurt. Go back to your work now and maybe we'll try again later."

The two ladies left as the doctor picked up a pen and turned his attention to a paper on his desk.

CHAPTER FIFTY-THREE

*D*rew picked Carol up at her apartment and programmed his GPS with the address Janice gave them. Carol had written the address of Lakeside Nursing Home on a note pad as well as the address of the home in Montevallo. Thirty-five minutes later they were driving up to Lakeside. They parked in front and took a minute to study what they were up against.

It was a formidable brick building with bars on the windows and a massive front door. It was plain, almost totally devoid of shrubbery. This was not an attractive facility and nothing had been done to make it attractive. It could use a paint job, at least. It reminded one of a prison rather than a nursing home.

The two walked to the huge wooden door and rang the bell, which could be heard echoing inside. After a minute, a deep female voice asked who it was. "We need to see Dr. King," shouted Drew.

"He's not available," said the voice.

"Then we'll wait until he is. Please open up or we'll be forced to call the police," said Drew.

There was a long pause before the voice said, "I can't open this door. Please drive around back. Someone will meet you there."

"The police threat did it," Carol said. "They might just be afraid of the authorities." They drove around to the back door where a man in a dark suit met them at the second door.

"I'm Dr. King," he said, extending his hand to Drew and then to Carol. "And who are you?"

"I'm Drew and this is Carol," Drew said, eyeing the doctor.

"How may I help you?" King asked.

"We're looking for Kathleen Larson, whom I believe is housed in your facility," said Drew.

"We don't have a Kathleen Larson in this facility. You must be mistaken," King said with an exaggerated grin.

"We would like to see for ourselves," Drew said. "Mrs. Larson is my client and I'm responsible for her welfare. It has been difficult for us to find her, but we have information that she might be housed in your facility. We would bring her back home."

Drew was stretching the truth quite a bit, but he had no intention of leaving without searching for Kathleen. "We can get a warrant but didn't think we needed one," Drew added. He was surprised when Dr. King moved toward the door and told them to follow him.

It was obvious by the way that King allowed them free reign that Kathleen was not in the facility. He was most happy to open every door and invite them to see for themselves. He took them to the administrative offices and opened the closet doors. He even took them into the kitchen and opened the walk-in refrigerator. They were able to observe the patients from behind the mirror and were then taken to each room. He showed them the roster of patients and Kathleen Larson's name was not to be found.

During the entire visit, Dr. King did not leave Carol and Drew alone to speak with the patients or staff. This fact caught Drew's attention. He suspected King didn't want them asking questions of someone who might just happen to know something.

"Doctor," said Carol while they were still in the common room, "we've made a terrible mistake. We're sorry to have accused you of harboring my mother-in-law. I know you understand my concern. She has been missing for too long now and we're concerned. We're sorry to have bothered you."

"We're happy to oblige. You say this Mrs. Larson is your mother-in-law?" asked King with an air of surprise.

"Yes, although her son and I have been divorced a long time. In fact, he is now deceased. We're sorry to have taken up your time."

"No problem. Call me if I can be of assistance," said King, somewhat nonchalantly. Drew handed the doctor a business card and was given one in return. "Maggie, could you see our visitors to their car?" he asked the nurse.

Maggie answered with a curt, "Yes, sir."

Maggie led them through the administration door, using the keypad. She led the way to the back door and out into the parking area, saying nothing. When the door closed and they were only feet from the car she said quietly, "They're missing. They were here but they escaped. I've got to go." Without another word, she turned and quickly retreated into the building.

"What do you make of that?" Drew asked.

"I think we found out where Kathleen was being sheltered. The only trouble is we don't know where she is now."

"I would like to talk with that lady to find out what she can tell us." Drew held the door for Carol. "I wonder what she knows. She said they escaped."

Carol and Drew left the premises and headed south toward the interstate. About fifteen miles down the road, they stopped at a convenience store for a cup of coffee. They sat at a picnic table on the store porch and rehashed their visit to the Lakeside Nursing Home.

"What do you think, Carol?" Drew asked, as he sipped his coffee.

"King is lying through his teeth. Did you hear how he reacted when I told him I was Mrs. Larson's daughter-in-law? He knows who Kathleen is because he thought Tillie was her daughter-in-law."

"And that nurse was trying to tell us they had been there but somehow escaped. Could she have meant Kathleen and another patient? Do you think 'they' were in the nursing home?" Drew asked.

"No. Dr. King was a bit too anxious to make sure we saw every room, closet, and nook. He wanted us to be certain Kathleen wasn't hiding in any one of them. No one was protecting any rooms or areas. It seems like he protests too much. He just wants to make sure we don't come back a second time," Carol said. "He even showed us the walk-in refrigerator.

Carol paused for a minute before she asked Drew, "Did you notice what a dismal place that was? There was no stimulation of any sort and the people walked around like they were ninety years old. Others were just sitting at tables, staring ahead. No one was reading and there wasn't even a television to entertain them. What a terrible place to live."

"I'll bet most of those patients are Alzheimer's patients or have serious dementia," said Drew. "King was not afraid of us talking to any of them. He did make sure we didn't talk to any of the staff, though."

"Yeah," said Carol. "He did make a mistake, however, when he let Maggie show us to the door."

The two finished their coffee and headed for the car.

"Remember, that nurse said, 'They were here but they escaped. They're missing,'" said Carol as she climbed into the passenger's seat. "She used the plural. That means Kathleen must've escaped with someone else."

"Maybe that's good," said Drew as he started the car. "Two heads are better than one and they might be able to help each other. That was the biggest mistake King made—letting that nurse take us to the car. Okay. We know where she was living, but not where she is now. Let's call Officer Rogers." He pulled the car onto the road and they headed back toward Birmingham.

CHAPTER FIFTY-FOUR

*I*t was fifteen minutes after Carol and Drew left that Alexander King requested Inez Lee and Maggie Pope come to his office.

"Inez, are you available to take me to that log cabin?" he asked. "I'd like to see for myself no one is living there. I understand there are very few homes on that ridge from here to the interstate."

"Doctor, I'm way behind and there is a lady in the infirmary who slipped and fell and needs my attention. Maggie knows where the house is. Maggie, could you take Dr. King?"

"I'd be glad to show you," Maggie said, exchanging a look with Inez.

"Meet me out back and we'll take the Chrysler," was King's curt response.

Paige and Kathleen were walking at a snail's pace when they saw the log cabin peeking through the bare trees in the distance. The sight gave Kathleen new energy to fight her pain and reach the cabin to sit down.

She knew her ankle was swollen and she shouldn't be walking on it, but what choice did she have?

"Hang in there, Kathleen. It's a few minutes away. Then you'll be able to get off that ankle," said Paige, patting her on the back.

"You have no idea how good that sounds. I wouldn't have been able to go another mile. Even a half mile might be too much." Kathleen strained to speak as she carefully took her next step.

"Here…we're almost there. I'm going to move ahead so I can open the window and get the front door open. That will save some time," Paige said, as she moved much faster toward the cabin.

Paige climbed through the window without help. She was now experienced at getting through the window by stepping on the log first. She opened the front door for Kathleen, and immediately locked it the moment they were both inside. "Take off your shoe and I'll see if there's some ice in the freezer. I saw a tray of cubes yesterday."

Kathleen tried to remove her shoe but couldn't reach her foot. She was sitting on one of the kitchen chairs. "Paige, I'm going to need some help."

"I'll be right with you. Let me break up this ice." A moment passed and Paige shouted, "Damn it! Now who the hell is that? Kathleen, get under the bed. I think that's Dr. King. There's a big black car coming up the driveway. Quick, Hurry!"

Kathleen did as she was told, locking the window as she got on her knees to roll under the bed.

Paige threw the ice tray back in the freezer and spent two seconds making sure she moved the chair back to the table and left nothing out of place. She grabbed Kathleen's walking stick and shoved it under the bed. Kathleen was already under the bed. It was a narrow fit. Paige, being thinner, had less trouble. Kathleen bumped into the stick and pulled it toward her so it wouldn't be seen.

"Now, Kathleen, we have to be very quiet," Paige whispered.

It was only seconds later when they heard someone try the door.

Maggie and Dr. King had driven in silence the eleven miles to the dirt driveway on the left of the road that led uphill to the log cabin. King welcomed silence from Maggie, so she offered no comments. This was King's operation and he was determined to find those two.

They sure had a lot of guts if they walked this far in one night, King thought. *In the dark, no less.*

King parked facing downhill, put on the brake, and before Maggie was out of the car, he was already on the porch trying the front door. He looked in the window on the right of the door, and the one on the left. He moved to the south side of the house and looked in that window at the bed and the bathroom that faced the window. Then he went around back and to the north window, looking into the kitchen and dining area. Maggie stayed on the porch while he investigated.

Dr. King stayed at the last window longer than the others while Maggie watched him. When he moved away, she walked around the cabin. What she immediately noticed was the south window was locked. King had noticed this also, but it only told him the cabin had not been broken into. Maggie knew at one time the window was not locked. *The women were inside!* She was sure of it.

Maggie wanted to shout out to warn them, but she bit her tongue. She was positive King would bring them back to Lakeside and lock them up again with no chance of escape. She didn't trust Dr. King and was sure they were safer inside. She looked behind her into the woods and saw a distinct trail leading to the window. It was unmistakable. If King wasn't so impatient and impetuous, he would have noticed it, too. He was already halfway to the car when Maggie came around the corner of the house, pleased he'd missed all the signs.

In the car, King finally wanted to talk. "It's obvious they didn't reach that cabin," he said. "It was all locked up with no signs of a break in. I didn't think they'd be able to walk that far, anyway, not those two old ladies in the middle of the night, in total darkness. If there was a moon that night, it wasn't much. Besides, I'm sure they had no idea where they were going and they couldn't make good time walking through the woods. They must be holed up someplace closer to Lakeside."

Maggie nodded silently as the car zipped down the road toward the nursing home once again.

Kathleen and Paige waited until the car was no longer heard in the distance. Then they painfully extricated themselves from under the bed. Paige held up a fist and Kathleen stared at it, not sure what she was doing.

"How about a fist bump?" Paige asked.

"What's a fist bump?"

"It's how the young people congratulate themselves. Get with it, Kathleen," Paige snickered.

"I'm with it all I want to be," Kathleen said, dismissing her with a wave of her hand. "Now if we can get out of here and back to safety, you might get your fist bump."

"I look forward to that. Don't worry. We'll get out safely. How about rustling up some grub, partner?" Paige's pleasant manner was contagious.

"Let me check the pantry," Kathleen said, hobbling toward the kitchen.

"No, you sit down and we'll get some ice on that foot. I'll find us something to eat."

Paige helped Kathleen get her shoe and sock off and observed that her ankle was more swollen than before. Considering all the walking they'd done, it was a miracle it wasn't worse. Paige put some ice cubes in a wash cloth and placed it on the ankle. Then she tied a plastic bag around the ankle to keep it from dripping, using two rubber bands to keep it snug.

In the pantry, Paige found a can of string beans. She put these in a sauce pan and warmed them. Both ladies were hungry and after nursing home food, it didn't matter what they ate. It was food. The string beans were washed down with tall glasses of cold water from the faucet. When they finished eating, Paige checked Kathleen's ankle and pronounced the swelling had subsided.

"Why don't we take a nap? We're both tired and getting off your feet will be good for you," said Paige.

"You don't have to convince me. I'm ready," said Kathleen, and within minutes, they were both asleep.

CHAPTER FIFTY-FIVE

*D*rew and Carol took Drew's car to downtown Homewood to see if they could speak with the two detectives assigned to Kathleen's case. Neither of the men was in the office, forcing them to leave word with a secretary. Then they headed back to Carol's apartment.

"Come on up and I'll make some tea," she said "It might be good to talk."

"Good idea," said Drew, as he followed her upstairs.

Once they heated the water, steeped the tea, and were seated and sipping, Drew observed, "So far, we've done more detective work than those who are paid for it."

"That's because we're closer to Kathleen and have a personal interest in finding her," said Carol.

"Carol, the second I hear anything I'll give you a call. I have a feeling we're getting close to finding Kathleen." Having finished his tea, he put the cup in the sink and walked to the door.

"I'll be waiting," she said. "Thanks, for taking such an interest in Kathleen. She's such a trusting person, anyone could take advantage of her. She now has a strong defender in her corner."

"And she has you. You're the heavyweight. I'll call when I hear something," he said, and made his exit.

After a moment, Carol decided she needed to talk with somebody about what she and Drew were able to uncover at the nursing home. Rudy came to mind and she dialed his number.

"Hey, Rudy. We just got back from a nursing home we think she was in."

"Did you see her?" he asked.

"No. But both Drew and I found their behavior suspicious. They were knocking themselves out to make sure we saw everything...every room and every closet. And they even showed us the walk-in refrigerator."

"And that was suspicious to you?" Rudy asked.

"It was. Then, as we were leaving, one of the nurses whispered to us as we were getting in the car, 'They were here.' Then she quickly went back inside. It was weird."

"I wouldn't count on finding her there," he said, dismissively. "Maybe they moved her or maybe the nurse was talking about someone else. Be careful about getting your hopes up." This negativity was just Rudy as usual, but Carol was having none of it.

"Look, Rudy, you weren't there," she snapped. "If you were, you would have seen and felt what we felt. Kathleen was at that nursing home but is no longer there. We don't know where she is, and I believe Dr. King doesn't either. But somebody knows something and when we get to the bottom of all this, we'll find

Kathleen." She wasn't about to let Rudy throw cold water on her visit to Lakeside Nursing Home.

"Okay, okay," said Rudy. "I wasn't there and I didn't experience what you experienced. I just don't want you to get your hopes up too high and lose your perspective. Look, Carol. I believe you learned something and maybe she was at that nursing home. But Tillie knows where she is and until we hear from her, we'll just have to wait." His tone was almost condescending, though Carol knew this was his best effort to be supportive.

"I'm afraid I can't wait that long, Rudy. I'm waiting to hear from Drew about what the detectives think. Talk to you later." Carol hung up without waiting for a response. Rudy was entitled to his opinion, but she didn't have to share it. And she sure as hell didn't share his negative thoughts.

Inez was called to the infirmary to attend a patient who had fallen and had deep contusions on her arm and hip. Inez didn't believe she'd broken anything, but without an x-ray, she wouldn't know for certain. When Dr. King returned with Maggie, Inez asked to see him.

"Can it wait? I'm busy now," said Dr. King.

"Maybe it can," said Inez. "Mrs. Monroe is resting comfortably and is sedated. I'm not in a position to say whether her hip or arm is broken. I need your opinion."

"If she's comfortable, stay with her and I'll be in shortly. I'm busy at the moment."

Dr. King is always busy at the moment, she thought *If it has to do with patient care, he's tied up. I don't think I've ever seen a doctor who cares so little about his patients. He probably doesn't even have the slightest idea who Mrs. Monroe is. I'll stay with her until he comes. She really needs an x-ray, but probably won't get one.*

Inez returned to Mrs. Monroe's bedside in the infirmary. She was asleep and the sides were up on the bed, making it difficult for her to fall out. Inez sat down in the folding chair next to the bed and listened to her patient's gentle snoring.

Maggie, hearing Dr. King on the telephone in his office, stuck her head through the infirmary door and saw Inez. "Inez, we need to talk," she said sternly.

"Bring a chair over here and we can chat," Inez said, not wanting to get up.

"No. I mean *talk*. I've got something to tell you," Maggie whispered.

"Does it have to be now? I'm tied up with a patient," said Inez.

"Inez, this is important." Maggie grabbed a chair and brought it over to where Inez was sitting. "I know where the two ladies are," she whispered.

"Are you sure?" Inez said, her eyes growing wide.

Before Maggie could say another word, Dr. King came through the door. Maggie was a bit flustered but managed to say, "We'll talk later, Inez. I need to go."

"What was that about? Did I break up something important?" King demanded.

"No, Doctor. She just wanted to tell me about her boyfriend," said Inez. "We can do that anytime."

"Well, it would be best if you did that on your own time and not company time," King said sternly. "We don't pay you to discuss your private lives while you're supposed to be taking care of patients."

Dr. King didn't get many chances to assert his authority; the nursing home ran perfectly well without him and didn't need him telling the staff what to do. After all, the patients were all sedated and no trouble to control. So, when the opportunity presented itself to boss a few employees around, he took advantage.

Inez directed their attention back to her patient. "Mrs. Monroe fell today and landed hard on her left side and arm. I put ice on both locations and the swelling is minimal, but the bruising is extensive. The hip doesn't hurt her too much but the arm is sensitive. I believe you need to examine her, Dr. King."

"Did you fill out an accident report?" He didn't wait for an answer but told her to get the form and fill out the report. "You do that and I'll examine the patient."

Inez couldn't remember a time when she saw Dr. King examine a patient. He always sent her away or had a task for her. She had long wondered if maybe he didn't know what he was doing and didn't want anyone to see how incompetent he was. And it was true; King knew he was incompetent but didn't want anyone else to know.

The report forms were in the administration office and Inez went there to get one. She was gone just several minutes before returning to the infirmary, and when she arrived, Dr. King had completed his examination.

"She'll be okay," he said. "The bruising is bad but I don't believe there is a fracture. Keep her in the infirmary overnight and have one of the assistant nurses stay with her. Have her call you if there are any problems. I would start an IV and have the assistant replace it during the night. Keep her sedated and immobilize the arm." King said all of this without making eye contact; he was always in a rush to be somewhere else.

Inez sat down at the table on the far side of the room and filled out the form. She made the incident appear like a minor event rather than the serious accident it was. She knew that would please Dr. King and he might reconsider his suspicion of her for the concern she'd shown the missing patients.

CHAPTER FIFTY-SIX

*M*aggie went about her job with one eye on Dr. King. She was looking for some activity that would keep him busy for a few moments. She didn't want to be seen talking to Inez after he believed she was spending idle time talking about her personal life. She needed to get Inez alone.

In the middle of the afternoon, King received a phone call. He left the phone visible on his desk as he opened his file cabinet. Maggie decided whatever he was engaged in would keep him occupied for at least a few minutes. She went to the infirmary to speak with Inez.

"Inez, I know where the two ladies are," she whispered.

"Where, Maggie?"

"They're in the log cabin."

"I don't believe that. We looked and they weren't there. The place was clean and neat. What makes you think they're at the cabin?"

"Remember that one window that was open? Well when I went there with Dr. King, it was locked. They must have been hiding under the bed or something.

After King went back to the car, I looked in the woods and could see a trail in the leaves. Dr. King didn't see the trail and thinks they are hiding some place nearer to Lakeside."

"Well I'll be damned," said Inez. "Those are two gutsy ladies."

Maggie nodded. "Look, Inez. I don't know what to do. And I don't want King to see me talking to you again. You know what he'll think. Tell me what you think we should do."

"Give me some time. I'll try to think of something. We can't just leave them there. Stay busy and I'll talk with you as soon as I can."

Maggie left the infirmary and busied herself with cleaning up the tables with disinfectant. It was a never-ending job that nobody liked to do. But for now, it took her off the hook and if seen, she might get some recognition for doing what needed to be done.

When Kathleen woke up, her partner was puttering about in the kitchen. She looked at her ankle and was pleased to see the swelling had subsided. She called Paige, "What's for supper?"

"How's my patient?" Paige said cheerfully.

"Pretty good, for an old lady. The swelling seems to have subsided and the pain has diminished considerably," said Kathleen.

Paige looked at the ankle and confirmed it looked better. "Look, Kathleen. I found some duct tape in the closet. I'm going to put a strip of cloth on your foot and then put the duct tape over it. That should give you some real support. The cloth will keep the tape from coming in contact with your skin. If it does, it will only stick to a small part. Occasionally, we just have to use what's available."

"That's fine with me. It sounds like a good idea. My ankle could use the support," Kathleen said.

Paige got the tape and cut a strip of dish towel to cover the ankle. Then she covered that with the duct tape.

"How does that feel, Kathleen? Did I make it too tight?" she asked.

"No, it feels good. I'll be able to walk on it, if I have to. It feels real good."

"Let's get a sock and shoe on and see what's left to eat."

There wasn't much left in the pantry, but there was still enough spaghetti for a meal. There was a jar of black olives that hadn't been opened and a can of corn. Half a jar of sauce was still in the refrigerator, just enough for a spaghetti dinner. Paige busied herself filling a pot with water to boil the spaghetti and getting a small sauce pan to heat up the sauce. There was still almost a half-bottle of wine in the refrigerator, and that got Paige's attention. She got a small glass from the cabinet and poured half of the wine into the glass.

"We sure do well, don't we, Kathleen? How about if I add some olives, as a side dish, to our pasta?"

"You're the chef. Whatever you say."

Over supper, Kathleen brought up their situation.

"We're almost out of food and my ankle shouldn't hurt too much in the morning. I think we have a chance to find someone who can help us. If we stay off the road when employees from the home are coming to work, our chances of getting help from a local should be pretty good. Some people might be afraid to pick us up, but two old people shouldn't scare them too much."

"What if we make a sign? We could write 'Birmingham' on it or maybe, 'Need Help,'" said Paige.

"A 'Need Help' sign will do it. Let's see what we've got to write on," Kathleen suggested.

Paige checked the pantry and found several paper bags from Food World.

"Now I need a magic marker," she said. She started going through all the drawers and found one in the drawer with the wine opener, thumbtacks, a screwdriver, and a hammer.

Five minutes later, using the back side of a paper bag, Paige had drawn a sign that said in big bold letters, **NEED HELP.** "Do you think this will do?" she asked.

"I think it will do just fine," said Kathleen. "The lettering is neat. We may look like crazy people, but the sign is the work of someone who has fine handwriting. You did a great job, Paige."

"Thanks," said Paige. "I used to do quite a bit of artwork and I do have good handwriting." Changing the subject, she added, "It's a shame we don't have a television. If we did, we'd have a fine evening."

"Just being safe, having a companion, and being out of that crazy house satisfies me," said Kathleen. "In the morning, we'll get help."

"I'm beginning to believe we might get to safety tomorrow," Paige said.

CHAPTER FIFTY-SEVEN

*M*aggie finished disinfecting the tables in time to start moving the patients in for supper. A kitchen staff member rang the bell, indicating it was time for all the patients to find a seat. Many of the patients, as usual, didn't know where to go and just continued doing what they had been doing—that is standing and staring or sitting and staring straight ahead. Maggie and several other nurses gently led patients to the tables. There were no assigned seats and everyone got the same food to eat, so where someone sat didn't matter. Choices were not an option.

Eventually everyone had a seat and the big carts with the warmed-up suppers were wheeled out into the common room. A plate was placed in front of each patient. After all the patients were served, kitchen staff poured their drinks. Depending on the day, the drink could be milk, sweetened ice tea, or Kool-Aid. The assistant nurses, those dressed in pink scrubs, assisted by observing each table. If a patient wasn't eating, an assistant often helped them start by feeding them. They occasionally had to make certain one patient didn't steal from another, and all the nurses knew which patients were most likely to do that. When milk was the drink for the evening, some patients lacked the strength or dexterity to open the containers. That task also fell to those in pink.

Maggie was looking for another opportunity to speak with Inez. She knew in the fishbowl of the common room she might be under observation, and it frustrated her that she couldn't see who was doing what behind the mirrored wall. So, for now, she did her job and patiently awaited an opportunity. Several times she saw Inez cross the common room, but the opportunity to speak with her never presented itself. Maggie wondered if she should do something with the knowledge she already had. Finally, Inez waved to her to follow her into the infirmary.

"I have to stay here in the infirmary until seven," said Inez. "That's when a nurse will arrive to relieve me. Dr. King thought it best not to use an assistant nurse and let her have access to a phone, so, I called one of the ladies who substitutes on weekends. I'm certain he wanted somebody who didn't know about the two ladies who escaped. She will call me during the night if she has any trouble. Can you wait until seven, or do you want to go home with someone else?"

"Inez, I want to go home with you. We need to decide what to do with," she lowered her voice, *"that information."*

"At seven o'clock, when I get off, we'll go to the cabin and take those two ladies where they need to go. We'll need a flashlight," whispered Inez. "Can you think of anything else?"

"No. I'll feel a lot better knowing those two ladies are safe," said Maggie. "If Dr. King doesn't get fired over this, we will. If he finds out we rescued them, he'll be furious. We're doing the right thing and I'll sleep better tonight because we did. I'm a mess right now," she said, checking over her shoulder.

"Find something to do until seven o'clock and we'll do our good deed then. I need to get back to work," said Inez, and she patted Maggie on the arm.

The next hour moved unbelievably slow for Maggie. There was nothing to read and the patients were in their 'recreational period' as it was called. It was not a recreational time at all, just more of the same. Each patient stood or sat and stared. If a person had even the slightest amount of compassion, they would feel sorry for those who were sent to this hell.

At six, the bell was rung again and the staff encouraged the patients to find their rooms. The assistant nurses knew who needed help and who could find their bed on their own. Gently, they led them to their rooms and thirty minutes later, the building was quiet and everyone was bedded down for the night. Maggie suspected medicine may have been added to their evening meal, but wasn't sure of that. She knew for certain, however, that the patients were tranquilized with a pill in the morning.

As the staff members headed home, Maggie sat in the administration office and waited for Inez. She was hungry, so she went to the kitchen and got a roll to tie her over until her own supper time. She returned and talked with the lady who handled the night shift, Andrea, and the security guard, Kenny. Something told Maggie the relationship between those two was more than a working relationship.

Kenny asked Maggie why she was hanging around. She told him she was waiting for her ride. Then he surprised her when he asked, "Have they found the two missing patients?"

"Not yet. At least not as far as I know," said Maggie.

"I'll bet they won't find them alive," said Kenny. "They couldn't live in the woods this long unless they had shelter. When they find them, someone's gonna pay."

"Who do you think that someone will be?" Maggie asked, raising her eyebrows.

"I sure as hell hope it isn't me. They always look at security when something goes wrong," said Kenny.

"Well who was on duty when they disappeared?" asked Maggie, trying not to sound too accusatory.

"We don't know for certain when they disappeared," he said, waving his hands dismissively. "All of a sudden in the morning they just weren't here. Andrea and I weren't made aware of them missing until we came in that evening. Did someone take them or did they just walk out? We don't know for sure." Kenny had given the situation a lot of thought. He was concerned his name would be connected with the loss of the two women.

Maggie didn't answer Kenny's question but asked one of her own. "Do you think someone should have notified the authorities?"

"Hell, yes! The second he found out someone was missing; King needed to call the police. These people can't take care of themselves. I think King is involved in a cover-up and the longer he waits to call the authorities, the greater the chance of those two not being found alive. I can't figure his game," Kenny said with conviction.

"And you think they'll blame you?" Maggie asked.

"I bet they do...or will try to. They'll say we were on duty when they disappeared since those ladies weren't here for breakfast. Security always takes the rap when something goes wrong. What I can't figure out is why they locked the door behind them. That seems odd."

"I think the two ladies were trying to stick it to Dr. King. Maybe they wanted him to know they weren't crazy," said Maggie.

"Maybe they were concerned others would escape and they would be blamed," said Kenny.

"That's possible...but I'll bet they wanted King to know they weren't crazy and were being kept here against their will," said Maggie.

Andrea got up from her computer and came into the room where Maggie and Kenny were talking. "Kenny, you should keep your mouth shut. The less you say the better. Yours is the first head that will roll since that's what they pay you for. Shut up, keep the patients in, and don't allow any visitors." She looked at the badge on Maggie's uniform. "Maggie, is it? Kenny doesn't know what happened and I don't know either, yet we were the only two on duty that night. How they got that key is beyond me. And I can't figure out how they opened that door from the common room. They would have to know the keypad numbers. A patient with dementia couldn't operate the keypad." Andrea paused for a moment before she began again. "I'm sorry for the ladies; I hope someone found them and took them someplace safe. But the fact we haven't heard anything or been contacted by anyone leads me to believe they didn't make it. I hope I'm wrong." She returned to her computer after adding, "Kenny, get to work."

CHAPTER FIFTY-EIGHT

*C*arol was fixing supper and sipping on a glass of Chardonnay at five o'clock when Drew called, barely thirty minutes after he'd left. "I just got off the phone with Officer Rogers. He told me they didn't find out anything new."

"Of course not," said Carol. "He didn't talk with anyone and Tillie isn't telling him or anyone else anything. Did you tell him we knew Kathleen had been at Lakeside Nursing home?"

"He said we had no evidence...only a hunch. And what that nurse said was not enough to act on. Who knows what she meant?" Drew rubbed his forehead with frustration. "He told me he and his partner would go to Lakeside in the morning and see if they couldn't get some real evidence. He said if they stonewall him, he'll know we were correct. He said they'd like to speak with the staff. That was something we couldn't do."

"Well, that's better than nothing," said Carol with concern in her voice. "Maybe in the morning we'll know where she is. I sure hope so. Her being gone like this and not knowing where she's being kept is frustrating. It's been two days since they left, as best we can tell. They would be hungry and in trouble if they spent all this time in the woods. I hope we find something new tomorrow."

"Carol, I'll give you a call the instant I hear something."

"I know you will, Drew. I'll do the same."

Maggie had her coat on five minutes before Inez was ready to leave. The nurse who was called to stay the night with Mrs. Monroe arrived early, but Inez had to tell her what was expected of her and where everything was kept. Inez had written out what she should do and left her cell phone number with the lady, just in case.

"It's better you call me than Dr. King," said Inez. "He wouldn't take kindly to being awakened in the middle of the night and he doesn't know where anything is, anyway. Mrs. Monroe is sedated and should be fine until the morning. There is some medicine in that IV. I'll be back at seven. Andrea and Kenny are in the administration area if you have any questions."

Having finished her instructions she got her coat, picked up her phone in the basket by the rear door, and joined Maggie. "Got the flashlight?" she asked.

Maggie nodded as the two walked to Inez's car.

"I hope we don't scare those two ladies," Maggie said when they'd reached the main road.

"I hope they didn't find a shotgun or rifle in that house," said Inez. "We could be in trouble if they did.

We'll just have to take a chance they'll figure out who we are before they decide to take action."

"I'll bet they would put up a fight if we told them we were taking them back to the nursing home," Maggie added.

"I'll bet they would, too. Do you remember their names?" Inez asked.

"One is Paige and the other they call Helen Parsons. But I don't think that's her real name," said Maggie.

"Her real name is Kathleen," said Inez as she turned on her high beams. "Dr. King made a mistake at least twice calling her Kathleen."

"Then we'll call them Paige and Kathleen. When Kathleen hears her name, she'll be okay," said Maggie.

"Don't be too certain," said Inez, shaking her head. They drove on in silence, each with thoughts as to how they might help the escaped women.

Inez slowed the car as she neared the road leading to the cabin. She knew it would be difficult to find at night so she carefully watched the odometer. It was just a tenth or two tenths shy of eleven miles. Sure enough, there it was.

"Okay, Maggie. This is it. Remember, we're doing a good deed and those women will be grateful once they know we intend to take them home," said Inez.

They drove up the dirt road and parked the car in the circle but facing the cabin. Maggie turned the flashlight on as they got out of the car. They left the headlights on and both stood in the light so the two ladies could see them. Then Inez shouted, "Paige and Kathleen! We've come to take you home."

The two women had long since finished their pasta dinner. Paige did the dishes and cleaned up the kitchen. She still had about a half glass of wine, having poured what was left in the bottle. She was drinking it slowly, savoring every sip. She didn't want to get dizzy like last time. This time she only had one glass and the bottle was empty.

"Do you know what I'm gonna do when I get home?" asked Kathleen.

"Call your good daughter-in-law?" Paige guessed.

"Of course…but after that." She waited and when Paige didn't answer she said, "Take a shower. I miss my shower."

"And everyone will be grateful," Paige laughed. "I'll be happy to get out of these clothes. The only reason we can't smell ourselves is because we got so many layers of clothes on. I may just decide to burn them or throw them out."

They both chuckled and then, suddenly, Kathleen's expression grew serious.

"Do you hear that, Paige?"

"What?"

"I hear a car…coming up our driveway." Now they could both hear the crunching of the gravel on the road.

"Damn. Maybe the owners returned. It has to be someone who could find that driveway at night."

Kathleen went to the window and saw two women emerge from a sedan. They stood in the headlights.

"Two of the nurses from the home just pulled up. Should we let them in?" she asked, backing up a step or two.

"Find out what they want first. Hand me a knife. They're not going to take me back to Lakeside. No way," said Paige.

"Paige and Kathleen! We've come to take you home," called Inez.

Kathleen's jaw dropped as she whispered to Paige, "They said my name. My *real* name. That's the first time anyone from the home has used my name. And they want to take us home!"

"We're not going back to the home. Piss off!" called Paige to the voice on the other side of the door.

"No, we want to take you to your home in Birmingham," said Inez.

"I think we can let them in," whispered Paige. Kathleen nodded.

"Okay. You can come in," she said, as she unbolted the door.

Kathleen opened the door and the nurses were surprised to see their patients looking healthy, clean, and happy, apart from Kathleen's distinct limp. They hadn't been sure what to expect.

"Are you going to take us back to our homes?" asked Paige.

"Yes, that's what we'd like to do," said Inez with a gentle smile.

"How did you know we were here?" asked Kathleen.

"Well, it was Maggie here who figured it out," said Inez." She noticed the locked window."

Both women hugged Maggie and then Inez. "Is there anything you have to do before we leave?" asked Maggie.

"Yes," said Paige. "I want to write a letter to the owners of this cabin. They don't know it yet, but they saved our lives." Maggie nodded as she helped Paige find a pen and paper for her letter.

"Do either of you have a cell phone I could use to call my daughter-in-law?" asked Kathleen.

"I have one," said Inez. "Give me the number and I'll dial it."

CHAPTER FORTY-FIVE

"Hello?" Carol answered her phone, expecting it to be Drew or Rudy.

"Hi, Carol," said Kathleen, almost choked up with excitement.

"Kay! Are you okay?" she said in a high-pitched squeal. "Where are you?"

Kathleen wasn't sure where to begin. "I'm okay. Two of the nurses from the Lakeside Nursing Home found us and want to drive us home. Where should I have them take me?"

"Thank God you're okay! You could go to your house if you had a key. Tillie's in jail," Carol spoke quickly through her excitement.

"Good!" said Kathleen. Tillie would get what was coming to her.

"Tillie has your house on the market but hasn't been able to sell it yet. Besides, it's priced too high and she's not available to speak to her realtor." Carol was talking too much from sheer joy.

"Damn her," said Kathleen. She never should have trusted Tillie for a second. "Listen, there is a key in the shed on the ledge over the window. I used duct tape to keep it from falling. You'll see it if you want to get in the house. We'll have these two nice nurses drive us there. There is another lady with me—a friend—and she has no place to stay. She can stay with me until her situation gets cleared up. Fix up the guest bed, please."

"Who is the other lady?" Carol asked, realizing she must be the other part of the "they" the nurse at the home had described.

"She was my roommate in the nursing home and we helped each other escape from that awful place. Carol, we'll talk when I get home. Make sure the hot water heater is working as we'll need a shower. It will take about a half-hour or so to heat up. See you then," said Kathleen, and she hung up the phone.

Paige wrote a short note to the homeowners that read: *"Mr. and Mrs. Jones, We escaped from the Lakeside Nursing Home and found refuge in your wonderful log cabin. It helped us survive. Without your cabin, we might have died. Letter to follow. Paige Whiteman and Kathleen Larson."*

As they pulled out of the driveway, Inez made sure to sing Maggie's praises one more time. "Every day, both coming to the facility or going home at night, Maggie was hoping you weren't sleeping in the woods. She wondered how you were doing for food," she said.

"I was so proud of you two, finding a way to get out of Lakeside," said Maggie. "I didn't want them catching you and bringing you back. I hope the authorities shut the place down."

"They won't shut it down," said Inez, shaking her head. "They need a place for the patients. But I'm sure they'll put it under new management and that will be good for us. I have a whole bunch of suggestions that will make that place better. You ladies did us a big favor, too."

"Maggie, I have a special gift for you," Kathleen chuckled. "I want you to be the one to give it to Dr. King in the morning, just before the police arrive. It's the key to the big wooden front door. I've been carrying it around so King would know we outsmarted him. Maybe when the police knock at the front door, you could open it with the key and let them in. I sure would like to be there when that happens. In any case, the key is for you."

"That would be fun, Kathleen," Maggie said with a wide grin. "I'll tell you all about it if you leave me your phone number."

The nurses asked a lot of questions and finally Inez asked the question that had been bothering everyone. "How did you get through the door with the keypad?"

"I sat near that mirrored wall and pretended to be asleep," said Kathleen. "Each day I memorized another number until I had all four. None of it would have worked if Paige hadn't told me about those white pills in the grits. That kept us both sane."

"Yep," said Paige. "The hardest part was acting like we were out of it."

They were almost to Birmingham on I-65 and Kathleen gave directions to reach her house. When they arrived, they were met by a police car, an ambulance, Carol, Rudy, Drew, and several paramedics.

"How about that, girls?" said Kathleen. "We have a reception committee."

CHAPTER SIXTY

The ladies were overwhelmed with all the attention. First, Carol welcomed Kathleen and Paige home, having learned who Paige was. She thanked Inez and Maggie for saving their lives, and then, true to form, set about making everyone comfortable.

"Let's take care of what we need to do," she said. "First of all, we've picked up a few ham and cheese sandwiches at the grocery store in case anyone is hungry. I'll bet all four of you are! We also have some soft drinks in the kitchen. While the paramedics are here, let's get you both checked out."

Paige spoke up. "I duct taped Kathleen's ankle—a pretty bad sprain. You may want to take care of that," she said to one of the paramedics. "I do believe Kathleen and I are a few pounds lighter, but no worse for the wear."

"I would feel better if we took your vital signs to make sure you're okay," said the paramedic with a smile. "Then if we're not needed, we can leave."

The paramedics checked their blood pressure, pulse, and temperature. They were both pronounced to be in good condition, considering their ordeal. It was recommended a complete physical exam be performed in the next day or so. After Kathleen's ankle was bandaged, the ambulance departed.

Carol spoke with several neighbors who came out when they saw the emergency vehicles. They were all pleased to hear Kathleen was fine and would have a good story to tell in the morning.

The police took the two nurses into the living room and spoke with them. They were assured there would be many more questions in the morning, but for now the police just wanted to know the basics. The police took their phone numbers and addresses and told them not to go into work in the morning. Both women would most likely be asked to testify against Dr. King. They were also told authorities would take over the nursing home in the morning and do a complete check of each patient. Inez and Maggie both voiced their relief at the latter news.

"Officers," said Maggie, pulling the key from her purse. "If you don't mind, I have an idea."

After the detectives left and the nurses said their goodbyes, Carol made a pot of tea and the women joined Drew and Rudy at the kitchen table for some conversation. Kathleen told Paige she had some clothes that would fit, although they were not too elegant. She had a pair of sweat pants and a sweat shirt that would do for now.

"Kathleen, why don't you get those things and I'll take a shower before I join you for some tea," said Paige.

"And I have a guest room for you. Take your shower and save me some hot water," said Kathleen. She'd miss having Paige's company.

Kathleen left to get the clothes and a towel for her guest and Carol poured tea. When Kathleen returned, Carol said, "Kay, you're on stage now. Tell us what happened starting at the beginning. And don't leave anything out."

Kathleen explained how Tillie had falsely obtained her signature and taken her to the nursing home. She told them about the shot she'd received, the little white pills, the snoozing security guard—it was quite a tale. The experience was so vivid for Kathleen, she was able to tell the story quite eloquently. Paige joined them after her shower and said nothing until Kathleen left to take her shower.

Paige told a similar tale, emphasizing how they'd faked being zombies to keep from being tranquilized.

Even after Kathleen returned from her shower the questions continued. Rudy may have summed it best when he said, "Both of you may have just experienced the adventure of your lives."

Drew had been silent during most of the recounting. Finally, when there was a moment's pause, he chimed in.

"I managed to get a call into Anthony Robertson, Tillie's attorney. Tillie refused to tell anyone where you were being held, Kathleen. Carol and I visited Lakeside Nursing Home just yesterday and that Dr. King lied straight to our faces. When I called Anthony, he said he was thankful you were safe. He also told me Tillie would be spending a long time in prison, especially since she refused to speak."

"What about the power of attorney?" Kathleen asked. "What will happen to my house and car and whatever else she controlled?"

"We'll have the POA officially declared a fraud and everything will be restored. She was asking too much for the house, anyway, so she never even got a nibble. Fear not, we'll get it taken care of," said Drew.

Paige addressed Drew with a wink. "Young man, I might need the services of a bright, handsome young attorney. Do you know of one?"

"I think I might be able to be of service," Drew smiled. "Tell me, Paige, why were you in that poor excuse for a nursing home?"

Paige explained how her daughter had put her in the home for five thousand in the bank account. She was a drug addict and needed some ready cash.

"What kind of a nursing home would take perfectly normal people who didn't need to be there and lock them up, sedate them, and keep them from their family?" Drew asked.

"A nursing home with a greedy administrator who can find other greedy people like himself." Paige answered. "Dr. King cares little for people in general and old people in particular. He's a monster."

CHAPTER SIXTY-ONE

"*A*nthony Robertson?" said a voice on the phone. "Yes? Speaking."

"This is Winston Grump. I would like to officially notify you that Mrs. Kathleen Larson has been found and returned to her home. More information will follow once we have finished our investigation."

"Thank you," said Anthony, breathing a sigh of relief. "I will so advise my client."

Anthony didn't mention that he'd already been so advised, thanks to Drew. He sat at his desk with his chin in his hands for a few moments, contemplating what this would mean for Tillie Larson.

The good news was, she would not be accused of murder. Unfortunately, however, she'd played a game of roulette and lost. She should have taken the plea bargain while it was on the table. At this point, she'd have little or no chance to bargain and would be completely at the mercy of the court. Anthony surmised a jury trial would only make things worse; she would get absolutely no sympathy from a jury. No, her only chance would be a lenient judge with a perverted sense of justice. Her goose was cooked.

Anthony put on his suit coat and headed for the jail. He never liked going to the jail, but he thought today might be different. Tillie had spurned his advice, numerous times, and now it was his good fortune to tell her how foolish she'd been. Yes, he was going to enjoy giving her the news.

"Tillie, I have some good news," Anthony said cheerfully. He was enjoying this moment.

"Oh. And what is that?" asked Tillie, hopeful that she was finally about to receive her reward.

"They found Kathleen Larson...alive and well. Lucky for you, you won't have to serve a life sentence. Congratulations!"

"How is that good news? How does that help me?" asked Tillie, almost shouting.

"You repeatedly ignored my advice and took a chance your mother-in-law would not be found. Despite my warnings, you just assumed charges would be dropped against you. That was a bad decision...a very bad decision. You were advised numerous times you were making a mistake. If your mother-in-law had been found dead, you would be facing a much greater sentence. You'll be spending a long time in prison, but probably not life. Come on, Tillie. That has to be good news."

"Get the hell out of here! Guard," she shouted. "Guard! Take this son of a bitch out of here!"

Anthony turned away, didn't say another word but waited for the guard. He had the slightest smile on his face.

Dr. King was cursing Inez Lee. He'd asked one of the nurses to come to his office along with the nurse who'd spent the night taking care of Mrs. Monroe.

"She hasn't showed up for work and it's after nine," he growled. "Where the hell is she? We can't run a nursing home if people come in any time they wish. This is not like her. She's always so dependable. And Maggie is also late. Damn it." In frustration, he got up and stood behind his chair. "Have them see me the moment they come in," he continued. "How is Mrs. Monroe?" he asked of the night nurse who was now tired and anxious to go home.

"She slept well last night," said the nurse. "She woke up complaining about her arm and hip. That's to be expected."

"We need Inez to handle her from here," said Dr. King. "She's responsible for Mrs. Monroe. Where the hell are they?"

Shortly after nine the first police car pulled up to the front of Lakeside Nursing Home. A second pulled around back, three other patrol cars parked in the parking spaces in front. A caravan of black sedans and white SUVs parked on the shoulder of the road along with several emergency vehicles.

Captain Palmer of the Homewood police squad led Maggie and Inez to the big front door and rang the bell. A voice told them to go around the back, but Maggie put the heavy iron key in the dead bolt and turned it. The officer pushed open the door.

"Good morning," said Maggie to the nurse in white. "We're here to see Dr. King."

The nurse was rather surprised and didn't know what to say. "Who may I say is calling?"

"Tell him, Captain Palmer of the Homewood Police would like to have a word with him," said the officer. "Please take us to his office."

Captain Palmer was accompanied by a Shelby County Sheriff's officer who didn't say anything, but looked intimidating due to his size and demeanor. His presence was to prevent any jurisdictional problems since the home was in Shelby County. Captain Palmer carried a warrant from a judge in Jefferson County. Inez and Maggie followed, both dressed in white uniforms,..

When Captain Palmer reached Dr. King's office, the doctor was on the phone. The captain walked over to the phone and pressed down on the receiver.

"Dr. King, you are under arrest for participating in the unlawful detention of Kathleen Larson and the unlawful detention of Paige Whiteman," he said, dropping the warrant on King's desk. This was followed by a recitation of Miranda rights, before he put cuffs on King and turned him over to a deputy.

Inez and Maggie were brought to King's office and provided the captain with official testimonies as well as names of whom to contact for further information. King's office would be used as a command post.

When the medical staff arrived, the common room was turned into an examination station. A crew installed dividers for privacy and reviewed medical records along with records of what drugs each patient was taking. A retired doctor who had operated a nursing home for over thirty years was asked to fill in for a few days until things were under control. He personally examined each patient, and spoke with the nurses and assistant nurses to make lists of recommendations.

With the help of Inez, Maggie, and many of the other staff members, ideas were solicited and suggestions put forward. A detective was assigned to stay with the new doctor for the time being, and was instructed to question the security guard and night manager. A team was assigned to retrieve King's files before his staff could shred or destroy any documents.

By noon, things were returning to normal, or at least the excitement level was returning to normal. Lakeside was getting a full makeover and the first day had gone well.

CHAPTER SIXTY-TWO

*P*aige was staying with Kathleen until her situation could be remedied. Her daughter had skipped town, they believed temporarily, and was using Paige's credit cards as her own. The police were trailing her daughter's purchases and would soon have her in their custody. In the meantime, Paige's house was being monitored.

Drew obtained a court order from a Jefferson County Judge to overthrow the Power of Attorney and restore all previous conditions. Tillie Larson's bank accounts were seized and her assets temporarily frozen. This provided the necessary time to make restitution for Kathleen's items that were already sold. This included Kathleen's beloved Buick. Tillie had sold the car for a few hundred dollars, but, as Drew explained, it was worth much more than that and the difference would be withdrawn from Tillie's account.

According to Drew, Tillie was not cooperating with her attorney and the judge was reluctant to appoint an alternate attorney. The judge had informed Tillie she was being adequately represented and a new attorney would not give better advice than she was currently receiving. He gave her several days to withdraw her request.

Dr. King was denied bail after pleading not-guilty at his arraignment. The judge considered Dr. King might be a flight risk; he had family ties in Grenada and was apparently a veterinarian, not a medical doctor, and unfit to run a nursing home. King also apparently had bank accounts in the Cayman Islands and many business friends throughout the Caribbean.

Shelby County Health personnel were busy examining the patients at the Lakeside facility. Food was upgraded, the white pill was eliminated, televisions were placed in the common room, reading materials in the form of paperbacks and magazines were made available, and the nurses spent time interacting with patients instead of watching them from behind a mirror. Inez was asked to determine how many more staff members were needed. She received a pay raise for her cooperation, and was further requested to work out a schedule that would be more suitable both to patients and staff.

The night manager, Andrea, had a lot of information she was willing to share with the investigators. She had been instructed to send money to various accounts, known only to her as numbers. There were three accounts to which she sent a substantial amount of money each month, alternating between the three. These payments were listed as expenses in the accounting books. The payments would be difficult to trace as they were all written off as groceries, medical supplies, and operating expenses. Dr. King even had Andrea make phony receipts for those items in addition to real expenses. The numbered accounts were in the Cayman Islands, according to those doing the investigation, and a password was all that kept them from being returned to the United States. It appeared each account held upward of four hundred thousand dollars. Andrea was appointed an attorney who advised her to cooperate to the fullest if she didn't want to spend time in jail.

Security tapes confirmed that Kenny and Andrea were, in fact, conducting a romantic affair, but that was of little consequence. Kenny was fired for negligence, though he didn't appear to know about all the corruption and embezzling Andrea and King perpetuated every night.

Andrea confirmed his innocence in the matter. "Kenny's as dumb as wood, but sometimes that wood can be good when you work a job that's as dull as mine."

It was ultimately decided that Andrea was just doing her job and was not profiting from the illicit accounting work.

Inez was promoted and given administrative duties, bordering on what Dr. King's previous responsibilities. A temporary accountant was sent by the county to straighten out the mess and Inez was told someone would be permanently assigned in several weeks. Maggie was made head supervisor of the assistant nurses and was soon able to buy her own car—though she still preferred to carpool with Inez from time to time.

CHAPTER SIXTY-THREE

One week after they were rescued, Kathleen called Paige at home. Paige's daughter had been found and was resting comfortably in a jail in Knoxville, Tennessee. "Paige, how would you like to throw a party?" she asked.

"Count me in. You know I like parties."

"I would like to thank everyone who had a part in rescuing us. I want to especially thank Inez and Maggie," said Kathleen.

"I would, too. When can we do it?"

"I was thinking Friday night."

The two talked for a long time about their party, who would call whom, when they would get together, what they would have for refreshments, and what they would drink.

"Kathleen, do you think Carol and Rudy could pick me up and drop me off after the party?" asked Paige. "I want to have a few drinks to celebrate. Don't worry—I'll bring my own wine," she chuckled.

"Sure, I don't see why not. They only live a few miles from your home. If you wish, you can stay here. It's up to you."

"I'd rather sleep in my own bed, if I can," said Paige.

Both ladies enjoyed planning the shindig and calling those who were invited. The party was scheduled for eight o'clock the following Friday evening.

On Friday night, Paige arrived with Carol and Rudy, followed shortly by Maggie and Inez. They were joined by several of Kathleen's neighbors and at last Drew and his date, Nicole.

When everyone standing in the kitchen with a glass in hand, Drew proposed a toast. "To some of the finest people in our town. To our two nurses, who were the heroines in this drama; to Carol, who was determined to find out where her mother-in-law was hiding; to Rudy for supporting Carol; and to two very brave women who showed us and the city what they were truly made of. To Kathleen and Paige."

Everyone raised their glasses and soon they were all talking at once. This was not a shy group. Nicole fit in just fine, having heard all about the abduction, search, and rescue from Drew. She was thrilled to meet the two ladies who rescued the women and to meet Kathleen and Paige. They moved into the living room where snacks were placed on the tables. The only people who knew the whole story were Drew and Carol and so all others were interested in finding out what happened from the perspective of others.

At eight forty-five, the two detectives for the case arrived. They each asked for a beer.

"Officer Rogers, do you have anything you can tell us about Tillie and King?" asked Drew.

"Please, call me Jim tonight. And this is Harold Martinez."

"Ok, Jim," said Kathleen. "What is the latest on Tillie?"

"She hasn't decided if she will keep the attorney assigned to her or ask for another," said Jim. "The judge gave her a few more days to think about it and has told her it would be a mistake to switch attorneys. Her attorney is trying to get her to plea, but she refuses to admit she's guilty. She's looking at fifteen years of hard time for unlawful detention and she doesn't want to accept that. Strange, she was willing to put you away for life but doesn't want to do any jail time. She will also have her charges updated to reflect theft. She's a real piece of work."

"She made a big mistake when she wouldn't take the five-year plea bargain," added Martinez. "Now she'll do three times that. And she can't say her attorney didn't warn her."

"What about King?" asked Drew.

"He's in a heap of trouble," said Jim. "Two false passports were found in his apartment and he is wanted in Texas for a similar fraud. He is also known as 'Albert Ayuer' and 'Andre Mitchell.' They are doing an investigation of him in Grenada. Apparently, he studied veterinary medicine for two years but did not graduate. So, he is not even qualified to treat animals." Drew and Kathleen exchanged looks.

"He's not a doctor and was not qualified to be in charge of a nursing home," Jim continued. "We won't risk allowing him to make bond as he is definitely a flight risk and has relatives living in the Carribean. He's also hiding several offshore bank accounts. He'll be in jail for quite some time, if the judge has anything to say. The owners of the nursing home are being sued and will most likely lose their license."

Martinez chimed in, "Down at the station we are getting a lot of praise for solving the mystery of Kathleen Larson's disappearance. We didn't even know Paige Whiteman was missing. What we keep telling everyone is that the real heroes are Maggie Pope and Inez Lee. They stuck their necks out a to help these two women." Everyone clapped at his words.

"And I want to tell everyone," Jim began, "that Carol Larson and Drew Stephens broke the case open when they visited Lakeside and told us they were certain Kathleen had been there." Kathleen patted her daughter-in-law on the back.

Jim continued, "But the two gutsy ladies who somehow managed to escape from that prison-like facility and survive two nights in the woods have made us all proud. This is why we are all here tonight. To Kathleen and Paige. There are a lot of patients at Lakeside Nursing Home who will be a lot happier because of you."

Paige stood up and took Kathleen's hand. "Kathleen, you promised if we made it home you would give me a fist bump. I believe you owe me one."

Kathleen rolled her eyes and gave Paige her promised fist bump. Everyone applauded.

"Wait until the folks at the Senior Center hear about this," said Kathleen, and she chuckled as she poured herself another cup of tea.

CPSIA information can be obtained
at www.ICGtesting.com
Printed in the USA
FFOW03n1812181117
43548541-42311FF